GUARDIAN

GUARDIAN

Eve E. Moore

VANTAGE PRESS
New York

FIRST EDITION

Published by Vantage Press, Inc.
516 West 34th Street, New York, New York 10001

Manufactured in the United States of America
ISBN: 0-533-11181-1

Library of Congress Catalog Card No.: 94-90312

0 9 8 7 6 5 4 3 2 1

For [illegible] and Eric,
I love you

CHAPTER 1

"Captain, we must contact the general before we move out. This area is packed with weasels. It's impossible for us to escape without assistance!"

The bunker had been pounded with multiple grenades and missiles during the night. Dawn had risen, but to the human eye it was difficult to differentiate between night and day. Thick smoke settled above the glowing fires throughout the campsite.

"Then get him now! It's not safe to sit here much longer."

"Yes, sir!"

The communications officer contacted the general without hesitation. The captain was given his personal assurance that an evacuation unit was on its way. Then, in one breath, one last glance at the smoky sky above them, their world exploded, their souls and memories left behind, their earthly bodies destroyed.

Through the smoke the evac unit passed overhead, not stopping or landing; the men aboard knew their mission was unsuccessful. The choppers passed over the black, charred land several times before returning to their base. No life was seen to exist.

His mind clear, his feelings intact, the memories of his life held his attention and made him unaware of the immediate reality. He could not see, only feel himself as an entity with no physical being. The bodily functions with which he was so familiar had vanished. There was something new he was unaware existed.

Calm, serene, the most comfortable feeling he had ever experienced flowed through his soul. It was as if he were walking through a door which had always been closed, with something or someone answering all his earthly questions. There was nothing he could do. He did not want to lose this feeling.

He began to see, not through his eyes, but through his soul. Everything that surrounded him was "white." Not a white room, not white smoke, only white, which held his soul, comforting it as if cuddling a newborn.

He asked himself two questions. Why can't I feel my body? Where am I?

As he felt around him with the strength of his soul, the captain realized that his life on earth had ended. He remembered the explosion clearly, not realizing that the scene had occurred after his death.

A tall figure approached, cloaked in black. The captain's body had been blown into pieces; the only portions of his "physical" being that remained were his skeletal hands and face. As the figure reached out for the captain's soul, the captain found that he was not frightened; he felt rather a pure feeling of being rescued.

The figure's fingers wrapped themselves around the captain's soul and carefully placed it within his cloak. The figure did not communicate with words, but a soothing feeling comforted the captain's awareness nonetheless.

Time did not exist. He did not know how long it had been between his death and where he now found himself to be. It could have been hours, days, or even years. He did not know.

Do you know where you are?

The captain could hear the voice clearly. He had no ears;

again, he heard with his soul. Should he answer? How could he answer with no means of communication? He then realized his thoughts had been heard by the mysterious voice. He chose to answer carefully. *I know I am dead. I do not know where I am, but I do expect to reach Heaven. Is this Heaven?*

No, this is Purgatory, the place for making amends for sins by suffering.

The captain hesitated for a moment. Purgatory? Why had he not heard of this place? He'd always assumed he would be placed in Heaven and that was all.

You need to know why you are here. Do you want to know?

Do I have a choice?

Yes.

What was his choice? What would happen if he said no?

Nothing.

How come I can't think without your hearing me?

This is Purgatory.

Why am I here? I want to know.

You must make a choice. You have been delivered to Purgatory by death. Your life, as you knew it, ended before your time. You must choose between Heaven and Earth.

How can I go back to Earth? My body has been destroyed; technically, I'm dead!

Your body is dead. You *are very much alive. You may choose to begin life again or you may enter Heaven upon my approval.*

What happens if I choose Heaven? What is Heaven?

That I cannot answer. You must choose first.

How can I choose when I don't know what Heaven is?

You know what life is like on Earth. Your soul knows what Heaven is.

What happens if I choose to live again?

That I cannot answer. You must choose first.

He was frustrated. Not knowing with what or whom he

was communicating made him uneasy. He trusted this entity, but he did not know what to do.

Do not be frightened.

How is it that I could make decisions before, and now I find myself confused?

Fate does not weave your destiny once you reach Purgatory or Heaven. You are now on your own.

What, or who, is Fate?

You do not know?

I know what the word "fate" means. I didn't know Fate was an actual entity.

On Earth you have no control over the direction of your life. Fate controls all. If you stray from Fate's plans, you will be driven back to the correct path. That is why you were able to make decisions regarding your life. It is difficult now because you control your own destiny and that, my friend, is something you have never done.

If I choose to go back, will I remember speaking to you?

Yes.

Will I remember my death?

It can be recalled.

Will I remember my life as I lived it?

It can be recalled. You will know how and when it is needed.

How long do I have before my decision must be made?

Time does not exist here. Fate will place you where you are needed when your decision is made. If you choose to go to Heaven, you will be guided by Gabriel.

Gabriel, the angel?

If you wish.

How do I contact you when I make my decision?

As soon as it is made, your soul will be guided in that specific direction. You need not speak to me again.

Is there anything I need to know before you depart?
As long as you have questions, I will answer.
I have no more.
Then I will go.

CHAPTER 2

"I feel fat!" Val stared at her figure laughing back at herself through the full-length mirror. Val was pregnant but she did not know it.

"Why are you gaining so much weight?" Cory teased her, trying to make her laugh and take her mind away from the mirror.

"Oh, be quiet!" Her grimace contained a certain anger, but her eyes laughed and gave her away.

In the beginning of this particular day, Val had urgent plans. She showered and set her hair. On the bathroom sink was a vial. The test was positive. Val stared into the bathroom mirror. In her mind she struggled to make a decision that she was clearly afraid to make.

As she dressed, she listened to the rushing water of Cory's shower. Val played out in her mind the different reactions that Cory might have to the news. She first pictured him leaving, then stunned, then hugging her. She hoped for the latter.

Cory dressed as he listened to the morning news. As the weather report ended, Val turned the radio off. "Cory?" Val wanted his full attention for her announcement.

"Yeah? What's up?" He seemed puzzled but willing to listen.

Val turned to him smiling, hoping to soothe his fears. "We're going to have a baby." There, she'd finally said it. She felt confident.

Cory was frozen. His heart pounded louder than his own thoughts, which were racing through his mind.

"Are you all right?" Val wondered if she'd been right. She wanted to kick herself for telling him so abruptly. Cory read this in her eyes and decided to be calm for Val's sake.

"I'm fine. It's just a shock to hear. Please forgive me for my initial reaction. I'm very pleased, believe me! I just wasn't prepared to be a father so soon."

"Cory, I'm no expert at mothering either. We'll adjust somehow. Someone knows it's time for us even if we don't."

"When is the baby due?"

"I won't be sure until I see my doctor, but I guess I'm slightly less than two months along."

Cory was instantly silent, thinking of something Val could never guess. She wondered where his thoughts had traveled to. He began to speak, relieving Val of her curiosity. "Do you remember how funny the dogs were acting? It was about two months ago. Remember sitting down for breakfast that one morning and watching the dogs sniff a specific spot on the floor in the living room? I remember now. They both jumped and began sniffing as if something had just popped down between them."

"I remember, but I thought they were just startled by a sound or something like that. They did look funny sniffing the floor for as long as they did." Val stared at the floor as if her memory was playing out the scene within the floor design.

"This is strange. Now I remember that I've just been seeing things out of the corner of my eyes. It's still happening and has been for a while. Every once in a while I'll be walking through the house and something catches my attention. I'll turn my head to see what it is and there's nothing there." Cory began to laugh, realizing how strange he was sounding. "Do you think we have a ghost?"

"There may very well be." Val was disturbed by Cory's description of seeing things that were not there, as she had been experiencing the same phenomenon. "Why didn't you tell me earlier? I've had the same things happening to me. I thought I was losing my mind."

"I didn't want to mention anything because I thought I was losing *my* mind." Cory made Val laugh along with him. Then they discarded their conversation and continued the day as though nothing unusual had occurred.

The next few months went by quickly, but Val felt as if time was not moving. Her figure became wide and plump. Cory reminded her every day that she was pregnant and not fat. It seemed to make her feel better, yet when she stood in front of the mirror each morning, her self-esteem would diminish.

They each continued to "see things" but did not discuss the subject openly. Val mentioned to Cory one day that she realized that she had begun to wear her cross every minute of every day since the beginning of her pregnancy. Neither of them could understand why. Val had always kept her cross in her jewelry box, safely tucked away. This topic was one more oddity that was not discussed any further. Also, neither Val nor Cory could figure out how Val had gotten pregnant, as they had been very careful for the past six years.

The baby was doing fine and Val had never been healthier in her entire life. She was beginning to feel better about herself in her eighth month, realizing she was not going to be pregnant forever. She only removed her cross when she showered, but she kept it on the counter to keep it close by.

There was one particular night that Cory and Val would never forget. It was midweek and both dogs were sound asleep on the living room floor. Cory and Val were watching the news on the television as they relaxed after a busy day at their jobs. Suddenly, one of the dogs jolted awake and "watched" something move around the room. Cory glanced at Val and whispered to her to watch the dog. They both were careful to keep silent as the dog continued to appear to watch something.

A few minutes later, the dog stopped and went back to sleep. Cory and Val realized that there was something strange happening in their house, but they did not wish to find out what it was. "It" did not seem to harm anything, so they decided it was better to leave the subject alone and ignore it.

The day they were both waiting for had finally come. Val was three days early, her contractions ten minutes apart. Sprawled over the couch she survived the next contraction. Two hours later, the contractions were one minute apart.

Cory called the doctor immediately. The doctor's service answered his call, forwarding the urgent news. As Cory waited for the doctor to return his call, he watched Val going through multiple contractions. They were not giving her much of a chance to breathe.

Cory picked up the telephone on the first ring. "Hello?"

"This is Dr. Camilo. How far apart are her contractions?"

"They've been one minute apart for about an hour, I'd say."

"If they were one minute apart, she'd be in constant pain."

"Believe me, she is!"

"Well, for now, call the service when they're three to five minutes apart. I'll check back in a few minutes if I don't hear from you."

"Thank you." Cory replaced the receiver quickly so he could tend to Val. The contractions were still one minute apart, maybe not even that long.

A few minutes later the telephone rang again. "Hello, this is Dr. Camilo. Are the contractions still coming that fast?"

Cory was worried, but he was in better shape than Val. "Yes. She's in tremendous pain."

"Take her to the hospital. I'll meet you there."

Cory rushed through the house gathering Val's suitcase and pillow. Val had been constantly returning to the bathroom all morning. Now she struggled to get her sneakers on while another contraction was coming in fast. She knew she had to make one more trip to the bathroom before they left the house. She had removed her cross, leaving it on the bathroom sink.

It was a half hour's drive and a very disturbing one for Cory. He tried to concentrate on driving and comfort Val as each contraction came. When they reached the emergency room, they both chuckled as they searched for the entry door. Val was rushed to the labor room, while Cory admitted her. Most of the paperwork had been completed beforehand, making his job quicker. He was in no mood to fill out dozens of forms.

While the doctors examined Val, she writhed in pain as the contractions kept coming quicker and stronger each time. Her water had to be broken and an IV put in. The baby's blood pressure was below 100, making the doctors concerned. Minutes later, by giving Val oxygen, the baby's blood pressure rose to 123. The baby was out of immediate danger.

Cory entered the room as the doctors comforted Val and reassured them both that everything would be fine. It was too late for any painkilling drugs; Val had to do this on her own.

Dr. Camilo entered, half-dressed in his gown. He examined Val quickly. "Take her into delivery. She's ready to go."

They rushed her into a larger room where a huge table stood, with the usual stirrups for her feet. Val had always hated "spread eagle" jokes.

Val was rolled onto the table as she went through another contraction. She was told to push as hard as she could. Dr. Camilo prepared the area for the oncoming delivery. His assistant was close by, grabbing the necessary instruments.

The baby was coming fast, and this worried Dr. Camilo. The baby's head was too large for the opening. He grabbed a scalpel and proceeded to give Val an episiotomy, larger than normal for the baby was in trouble and they had to get him out.

As the head began to emerge, Dr. Camilo sighted a serious problem. Wrapped around the baby's neck was the umbilical cord. The doctor knew that he had to act fast or the baby would surely die.

CHAPTER 3

What will I become? The captain often asked himself questions, and this particular one came up often. It was a difficult decision to make. He wondered about Heaven. *What is it like? Will I be doing something? Will I be myself or something for which I am totally unprepared?* He looked around himself at the whiteness. White everywhere. He was not standing for he had no feet. He was just there.

So, were you told to make a decision? The voice came from an empty space, one that was a part of a man, yet it was submerged below thought. It was a very mysterious, low voice, almost soothing to a point.

Who are you? The captain was nervous. This being was nothing like the entity he had met earlier.

You may make a guess, but alas, you will never figure it out.

Why do you seem so confident?

I am confidence. I am also cunning, wit and charm. Do you know who I am?

No. I will if you are kind enough to give me more clues.

I am not kind.

How can I find out who you are if you give me no clues? Do I want to know who you are? Why is it so important? Go away.

I am always with you. I cannot leave.

Then stop speaking to me! You are needlessly harassing me!

Right.

Right what? The captain became aggravated and annoyed at the entity. He asked himself why should he care when he couldn't figure out who or what it was?

Because you must make a decision and I am here to help, the entity barked.

You are lying.

You, my friend, are correct. I am a liar.

I feel stupid. The captain was stunned. He began to piece together this mystery set before his eyes. The entity was giving him clues, although they were not outright stated. How could he have been so stupid? The entity was the Father of Lies.

Congratulations! You win a car, a mansion, and a yacht.

Oh, funny, aren't you? the captain challenged his uninvited guest.

If you choose to fight, you must be prepared.

Give it your best shot! the captain roared, defying the most dangerous parts of every soul—temptation, greed, and competition.

The sky turned blue, a beautiful warm sun was added, followed by several seagulls flying overhead. The captain found himself on an island. He could not determine the means by which he had returned to his physical body, but he recognized it as a ploy. *This cannot be real!* He comforted himself with the thought.

On the island were many palm trees. In the distance there was a waterfall, which tempted the captain to feel the cool, soft water. An abundance of colorful fish swam in the pool below the falls. As the captain stepped carefully on the sharp rocks above the water, he heard a voice behind him, a woman's voice, deep yet soothing. He could not comprehend the words, only bask in the calming waves of her tone. She spoke in musical notes, a beautiful song if heard with open ears. Then the voice vanished as if cut off with an axe.

He returned to his journey across the mysterious pool of

water. Glancing down into the pool, he watched his reflection distort as each ripple of water splashed against the rocks. What was he doing here? What was this place?

His attention was interrupted as a tall, voluptuous woman walked out from beneath the falls and stood before him. Her hair was jet black, long and shining. She was naked except for a row of leaves placed seductively around her head.

Do you wish me?

What? The captain was not prepared for her to speak and did not actually hear her.

Do . . . you . . . wish . . . me?

Don't be sarcastic! Who are you? No, I do not wish you. The captain realized that he had just turned down a beautiful, naked woman. Why? He did not trust her, at least for the moment.

Sorry. I do not mean to disturb you. May I tempt you?

Why? Who are you?

Yours.

Mine? I do not need you.

You need me to make your decision.

Explain. He was becoming curious, wondering what kind of test this was.

If you decide to go to Heaven, this is what you will see. I will be by your side when you need me. I am your thought. That's how Heaven thinks. If you want something, just imagine it and it is yours.

I do not think Heaven is a place for those kinds of thoughts.

Oh, but yes! You may think anything in Heaven! Isn't that what you have waited for? To be in Heaven and do whatever you please?

Why do you want me to go to Heaven? You are not there, you are only a thought. Right?

Yes, you are correct. I am only a thought, but I am your *thought. You make Heaven what you want it to be.*

She was beginning to make sense although the captain was wary of her. He did not trust her completely and could not comprehend why he had to trust her. *I do not believe one word you speak.*

The captain stood still as he watched the woman turn away from him, disappearing through the waterfall where she had first appeared. The palm trees that surrounded him faded, followed by the island, sky and sun. His body faded slowly, leaving him feeling as if he had died again.

White. It appeared again, reminding him of the decision. He felt somewhat relieved that the evil entity had left him alone. He did not need to be persuaded. He began to feel that for some unknown reason, something or someone did not want him to return to Earth.

As he sat pondering the situation, the scene around him began to change. Suddenly the ground beneath him was piled with garbage—bags, cans, uneaten food. A building emerged slowly, revealing broken windows and eroding walls. The sky was filled with dark, smoky clouds. He knew that it was daytime, yet it was difficult to see the sun.

He heard voices in the streets, hidden voices of children. The cries of hunger and pain filled the air as he proceeded to walk toward an old church at the end of the sidewalk. The doors hung open, partially off their hinges, as if they were stricken with disease, never to recover.

There was a dim, shimmering light within the pews. He walked slowly up the few stairs that were still intact. As he entered the church, the soft, soothing voice returned. The captain tried to hear what it was saying, but the words were muffled. The soft, musical tones whispered to him throughout the cathedral ceilings.

In the front pew sat a child dressed in rags, obviously hungry and dirty. The child slowly raised his head, concentrating on the crooked cross above the pulpit.

What are you doing here? Don't you have a home? The captain was genuinely concerned for the little boy, hoping he could save the child from whatever tragedy had caused him to be the way he was.

This is my home, sir. The boy replied in a gentle voice that was followed by a hoarse cough.

Where are your parents? He began asking the boy questions, hoping to find out where he was.

I have no parents. They were killed by the disease.

What disease?

Can't you smell it in the air, sir? It's staring you right in the face. The boy became alert, his voice controlled. *It's death, sir. The air is contaminated. Even I will die soon, that is why I am here at the church, my home.*

What has happened?

Where have you been, sir? It's the final World War.

Final?

Yes, sir. There is a total nuclear war. The world has been blasted to bits. Any land not directly hit gets the disease, which comes from the air. Every living thing will eventually die. Lucky us, huh, sir?

When is this? Is it in the future or the present? The captain was concerned. What was this boy leading to?

You will be born to this, sir, if you choose to go back to Earth.

So that was the ploy. *It can't be real! It has to be something I have imagined. That's it! It's my imagination and it's not real! I can make it whatever I want!*

You are lying! This is only an image from my thoughts! Someone is playing a very nasty game! The captain yelled at the sky, as if he knew that someone was certainly listening.

White. The captain was proud of himself for not giving in to evil. What was next? Should he make his decision now? Would that free him of these thoughts being played out, ingenious as they may be?

Thank you.

I did not mean that as a compliment!

Even if you do make your decision now, it will not stop me. I cannot touch you in Heaven, but I can, let's say, visit you on Earth.

I will fight you all the way! I have just made my decision!

Suddenly it was black all around him. A tiny flash of light passed near him, sounding as if it was sizzling and hot. The light stopped and began to glow. The captain was pulled near as he heard a melodious woman's voice coming from the light. He floated toward the light, realizing he was on his way to becoming human again. How, he did not know.

As he closed in on the light, his thoughts vanished. He remembered everything that had happened in Purgatory. His only memories, which would be with him always, were of his previous life. All in life that he had learned, loved, hated, and who he was as a person, he would never forget.

CHAPTER 4

You have entered the light.

I thought that was what a person did when he died. They always told me, "Walk toward the light."

It is true. You are to be born today. The parents have been carefully chosen, visited on several occasions to ensure your future.

Who are you?

You need not know, it is of no importance. There was a short pause; then the voice came again. *There is a problem. There has been some foul play during your period of growth within your mother. At the moment you are transferred, you will be tested. An evil entity has begun to strangle the infant with his own powers. You must stop him or the child will die and you will not live again. The doctor has also been carefully chosen, he is your tool.*

Tool for what? Why is an evil entity trying to kill this child?

Because you are the soul of this child and have been from conception. It is not known how the connection was made, but it is important that you be transferred immediately.

He felt a sudden rush of unbearable pain as he was transferred to the child. It was not extreme, only enough to awaken him. He could see through the child's eyes. It was a cramped space but he managed to figure out where he was.

I have a test for you! The voice came from above him. He could clearly hear and comprehend every word. *You must pass or the child dies!*

Name it! Somewhere he found the strength to fight this evil voice. Why was he being challenged?

You will find out soon enough! Now. You are prepared, my boy?

White. Where was he? A large mountain began to appear, bringing with it an ocean below. He was on a boat, alone and unsure of where he was. There was a sun rising from behind the mountain, glowing brightly and warm. He did not know the exact distance to land, but he guessed it was at least a few miles.

Another boat appeared. It seemed to drift on its own, no one at the controls and no one on deck. He decided to board the empty vessel, wondering why the ship was there.

There was no one in sight as he climbed aboard. The boat could have easily have held fifty men. Suddenly, he realized he was moving. The boat was bringing him closer to land, much faster than he could have ever paddled. Splashing through waves and riding with the wind, the boat began to go faster, as if time was an important factor.

Soon the beach appeared, and the boat drifted toward the shallow water, which would enable him to walk to shore. With his pants rolled high, he trudged through the water, realizing that it was a longer walk than he'd expected.

The sand beneath his feet was warm, inviting him to walk farther. He noticed that the tree line on the beach extended for miles; the mountain above was tall and mighty.

There were three shelters, made of palm leaves, spaced evenly. From the first hut on the left-hand side, an elderly woman appeared. The captain recognized her as his mother.

Oh, darling, have you come to stay with us?

He did not trust her, he had more sense than to think she was real. His mother had died shortly before he was shipped overseas to defend his country. As he remembered clearly, his life had ended patriotically. Not knowing where this episode was leading, he answered her question with another. *What are you doing here?*

She wore a deep brown housedress, covering her from her neck to her ankles, protecting her skin from the sun. She was as lovely as he remembered her. *Don't you remember, sweetheart? I'm not alive, I'm in Heaven. Your father is here too, see?* She pointed to the shelter closest to hers as the door opened, revealing his father dressed in his favorite suit that he always wore to work. It was the same suit he'd worn when he died. A sudden heart attack at this desk while at the office had taken his life too early. The captain was their only child.

Who is in the third hut?

Why, honey, it's yours if you choose to be with us. Don't you miss us? We've missed you dearly. She glanced at his father as if she was acting out a play written to deceive the audience. The captain was aware that she was not sincere.

I don't believe you're real! You're only in my mind! He wanted to run back to the boat and sail far away from this cruel joke being played on him, but he could not move. He missed his parents very much, and this awareness made his decision even more difficult.

Yes, I am in your mind and so is your father. Please join us now! She became impatient, her voice still sweet yet frustrated. This was not his mother.

No, I do not wish to be here!

White. He had returned to where he'd begun, knowing he'd passed the test.

You have won this time, but you will meet me again one day! The evil voice was gone, leaving in its place a pure feeling of love—the love of his mother-to-be.

CHAPTER 5

Dr. Camilo told Val to push harder than she ever had, hoping to save the infant from pain. As the cord was loosened, the baby came out quickly, Val watching every second of her child's birth. She was in the worst pain she had ever imagined existed; yet she was the happiest she had ever been in her life.

Cory was by her side throughout the entire delivery. He was a proud father and a loving husband. As he helped the nurse weigh his son, Val was being stitched up and prepared for her child to be placed on her chest.

Dr. Harbass, who'd assisted in the delivery, asked Val and Cory what their son's name was to be, purposely taking Val's mind off the pain she was experiencing.

Val replied, her voice cracking, "His name is Phillip." She smiled as Phillip was placed on her chest, allowing her to bond with him. She held him close to her, unable to look at each part of him, only his arms and head were unclothed. She gazed into his eyes, and he returned the look. They shared a love that few people experience. Cory was behind her as she lay on the table being stitched up.

The nurse came to take Phillip for his bath and warming. He was not yet adjusted to his new world; he was cold but warmed by the love of his parents.

The captain within Phillip realized now who owned the melodious voice present throughout his ordeal with evil. It was Val's voice he had heard, calling to him, giving him the strength to fight for his life.

The next few years were spent learning about life all over again. Phillip was becoming his own person, able to carry with him the captain's spirit, not knowing it was the captain who prompted him to cry when needed, laugh when his mother tickled him, and gaze in wonder at his father. Phillip would not know who the captain was until the time was necessary.

Val had hung her cross on the mobile of Phillip's crib the day they'd come home from the hospital. Oddly enough, Cory had seen her cross on the bathroom sink and brought it to her when he returned to the hospital on the evening of Phillip's birth.

When Phillip was two years old, Cory and Val took him to a pool, where they were met by several relatives of his mother's at a family reunion.

Val was busy gathering the empty dishes from lunch, while Cory, with the other fathers, watched Phillip. Phillip was a curious child. He was playing a game with an imaginary friend. His friend told him to follow, and Phillip did so immediately.

His friend led him around a tree and over a pile of leaves. Phillip was enjoying himself. Cory watched in amusement as Phillip walked around the yard, dancing and jumping. One of the fathers asked Cory a question, taking his attention away from Phillip.

Phillip's friend began to circle the pool, getting closer and closer to the edge of the water each time he passed. Suddenly, a splash was heard followed by several screams. Phillip had fallen into the pool and was drowning.

Cory quickly jumped into the pool to save him, knowing Phillip could not swim. Seconds later, Cory brought Phillip to the surface and swam toward the shallow end. Cory held onto Phillip tightly, not wanting him to slip out of his wet arms.

Phillip was all right after he was dried and rested. He slept for several hours, worrying Val and Cory as they watched over him as he slept. This was a day they would never forget.

Phillip grew faster as the years progressed. He was of medium height, with brown hair and deep, blue eyes. He was a handsome teenager. The girls were crazy about him, always calling him on the phone or "dropping by."

One night almost ended in disaster. Phillip had attended a party and consumed too much alcohol. He was legally drunk, but he offered to give a couple a ride home. He seemed to be sober, but he knew he was trying hard to control himself.

The boy and girl got in the backseat of his car. The three decided to go for a ride through the development by the cemetery to see the newly built homes. After they'd circled the streets for a while, Phillip had to relieve himself. They decided to stop and use the woods. Even the girl had to go.

Phillip turned into an empty, darkened lot, where it was impossible to see. He stopped abruptly. He thought it was the loss of a sense of direction that had made his foot jerk on the brakes.

Meanwhile, his friend jumped out of the car and headed toward the woods. Suddenly, he called back. "Phillip?" he said urgently.

"Yeah?"

"We're really lucky you stopped where you did."

Phillip slowly walked toward his friend at the front end of the car. Only inches away from the tires was a deep hole.

If Phillip had driven any farther, the car would surely have been smashed.

Four years later, Phillip again had too much to drink. Afterwards, he vowed never to have another sip of alcohol. While under the influence, he'd tried to take his own life. He was not successful, thanks to a friend he didn't know he had.

CHAPTER 6

The captain was kept busy during Phillip's teenage years, guiding him through romance and heartache, protecting him throughout every day, fighting the evil that wanted Phillip dead.

When Phillip had almost drowned, the captain had given Cory strength. But Phillip he'd found uncontrollable when put to the test. The captain had been able to order Phillip to apply the brakes and stop the car, when he'd almost driven into a pit, but he'd been unable to stop him when Phillip's "friend" turned on him. The "friend" told Phillip that he was unworthy of life. The captain still could not comprehend why this innocent child would be stalked by evil.

When Phillip turned eighteen, he announced he was enlisting in the air force. Val and Cory could not convince him to withdraw; he was set on his decision.

The captain was secretly proud of Phillip for his decision to enter the armed forces. There was never any persuasion on the captain's part. This finally put an end to his questions as to who was controlling Phillip's destiny; he was assured that the decision was Phillip's and not his own.

During Phillip's training, the captain guided him, knowing it would not harm anything. Phillip was exceptional in everything he ever did. He always followed orders and never got himself into trouble as his fellow bunkmates did.

He successfully completed his training and was assigned to an aircraft carrier to learn to fly with the best. His trial missions were completed within a few weeks. His superiors were confident of Phillip's abilities. He was ready for a long cruise on the Pacific, even knowing it was only a scheduled check mission. The aircraft carrier was set on its way to relieve her sister ship from a three-month tour of duty.

Two weeks into the cruise, Phillip was assigned to the first mission of the day. He had always flown daylight missions and was anxious to be over the sea at night. He loved flying under the moon as it danced upon the ocean waves. Phillip's co-pilot was concerned about the plane's condition. On their last mission, he'd noticed that the engine did not sound correct. Phillip assured him that the technicians had double-checked every inch of their plane.

They were given the okay for takeoff. Phillip always loved the feeling he experienced every time the plane entered the air and wished it would linger on.

As they followed their flight plan, they were careful to keep in contact with the ship. Phillip's co-pilot continued to show concern about the engine. Suddenly, the plane began to lose altitude. Phillip contacted the ship, alerting them to their danger. His co-pilot wanted to eject and Phillip agreed.

Phillip hit the water hard, almost drowning as the force of his fall pushed him deep into the ocean. His co-pilot was nowhere to be seen or heard, though he could have been hidden by the darkness of the ocean waves against the moonlight. Phillip was alone. He inflated his emergency raft and clambered aboard.

Whitman should have landed in the same area, but he was nowhere in sight. Phillip searched his pack for a flare, hoping to catch the attention of the aircraft carrier. He knew he would be rescued, but he did not know how long it would take.

Hang on. A search party is on the way.

Phillip heard the voice within him and wondered about it. He figured he was losing his mind and began talking silently to himself. *That was a close call. I wonder where Whitman is?*

Whitman is dead. He could not untangle himself from his parachute and drowned. You're lucky to be alive.

The voice was there again, this time answering his question. Now Phillip was really concerned about his mental stability. He had, on several occasions, thought over a problem in his mind, but his mind had never answered him before. He decided to play along, if only to stop himself from thinking about his present predicament. *How do you know Whitman is dead?*

I know.

It had answered him again! Phillip was even more confused, realizing he was having a conversation with someone other than his own mind. *Who are you?*

I am within you. Don't be afraid, I know I would be if I was in your shoes. You must listen to me carefully. Your raft will not last long. Then you must try to keep your head above water. For now, keep your strength up. Do not move around. You must rest.

Why? There's a search team coming.

They will not be here for a while.

Just as the voice faded, Phillip realized he was beginning to sink, along with the deflating raft. He began swimming in the direction of the ship. The voice kept him company until the helicopter's searchlight picked him out. The roar of the helicopter was loud; yet he had not heard it above the sound of the ocean waves crashing against his body. He was pulled aboard safely, thankful he'd only been in the water a short time.

"What the hell happened?" Phillip was outraged, first at

the technicians then at himself for not having listened to Whitman. "Whitman is dead, thanks to you!"

The supervisor was stunned, unable to answer as he wiped his sweaty palms on the back of his work pants, attempting to hide his uncertainty. The other technicians shuffled with nervousness. No one knew the answer to Phillip's question. There would certainly be an investigation conducted later on, but this did not satisfy Phillip. The death of his friend was devastating to him, as it was such an unnecessary death.

As a few members of the rescue team departed, Phillip informed the rest of the approximate area where the plane had gone down, hoping they'd find Whitman's body.

The question as to how Phillip could be so certain of his friend's demise came up the following day. He had no answer to give them. He just shrugged and responded, "Educated guess, I suppose."

Phillip devoted most of his time the following day to examining the plane, which the rescue crew had brought aboard. As he was looking at the engine, he found a slight cut in one of the hoses. It looked to him to have been made deliberately.

It had taken most of the day to find the problem with the engine, and Phillip suddenly realized it was dinnertime. He went to the mess hall. Several officers had already begun to eat. Phillip decided this was the best time to announce his findings. He chose two of his superior officers and took them aside, telling them his suspicions. The three agreed to inform the entire mess hall.

Stunned faces appeared at each table when the troubling announcement was made. The question of who could have done such an unlawful and despicable thing was in every mind. The announcement ended with an alarming statement. The ship would not return to base until the guilty party came forward. Whoever it was would be severely punished for his actions. There was no reason to hide; the person could not get very far unless he swam away.

Silent mutterings could be heard among the crew as they returned to duty for the evening. Phillip waited for the last of the personnel to leave the mess hall, hoping to be approached by the murderer of his friend. No one remained. Phillip was alone.

Now, boy! a voice bellowed in Phillip's mind.

Who are you? Phillip was clearly confused. This voice was different from the one he'd heard while in the ocean.

Alas, you may never know.

Why do you speak to me now?

My dear boy, you have been very lucky indeed. Poor Whitman. Such a tragic ending.

Who are you? Why are you speaking to me? Phillip paused, waiting for a response, but none came. *Who have you enlisted to do your dirty work?* Phillip was sure this voice he was now hearing was different from the other, but he could not determine why. Could it be the same voice?

Why do you assume I need help? the voice now said. *However, since you have asked so politely, I do have certain helpers who are of my own business.*

Phillip felt his anger rise. He was careful not to make it obvious. *I demand you tell me which man on this ship followed your orders!*

That is for me to know and you to not find out! It will ruin all of my plans for you.

Haven't you done enough? You've killed my co-pilot. How do you expect me to go along with your games?

These are not games. The voice was outraged, as if insulted. *I do not play games. This is real life, my dear boy. I have already shown you that clearly.*

Don't evade my questions! Name your real-life game.

Phillip knew he was taunting the voice, but he also accepted the fact that he was the one who was supposed to have died in the accident. It bothered him to know that Whitman had died before his time and he himself was alive. Who had saved him? He thought about the question deeply and did not at first hear the voice speaking.

. . . and if you cannot succeed, you will die, and I will have accomplished my goal.

Phillip was hesitant to ask the voice to repeat itself.

I know you were not listening, my dear boy. Remember, I know all that you say or think. Now, to inform you of your task.

The voice paused theatrically. Phillip imagined the voice smiling, reveling in its own ego. *There are three officers you must become acquainted with. The first man is Talreja.*

Phillip knew this man by sight, but did not know him personally. He remembered, however, Talreja's first day with the crew; it was a day which he would never forget.

Talreja had tripped and fallen overboard before the ship's engines were started. He was a new man, and the officers had all chided him afterward.

The voice seemed impatient, waiting for Phillip to stop his frivolous thoughts. *Talreja will be your teacher. The others are Manel and Lock.*

Phillip's thoughts raced as he suddenly realized that these three men were all new to the carrier and not part of its regular crew. His suspicions grew as the voice continued. *These men will help you to obtain my goal. Talreja will complete the final task. Find Talreja.* The voice did not speak again.

Phillip had been seated in the same chair during this conversation, and his legs had fallen asleep. When he tried to stand up, he slowly collapsed to the floor. He scanned the mess hall. No one had seem him fall. He laughed to himself and wondered how he was to explain the death of Whitman. He clearly could not blame it on a "voice" he had heard.

As he left the deserted mess hall, Phillip was curious about this so-called mission. He entered the bunk hall, tripping over an unknown obstacle as he made his way to his bunk in the dark. *Why does this thing want me dead?* he asked himself as he drifted off to sleep.

The captain was mystified. Why had this evil thing made direct contact with Phillip? He wondered whether he should speak to Phillip, clearing up the confusion he must be feeling. He did not want Phillip to distrust him when his whole purpose was to guard Phillip until the time came to leave him.

After long, careful thought, the captain decided to enter Phillip's dreams. He could show himself there and safely assume that Phillip would not be alarmed. What would the boy think? He must not know how or why the captain's soul was within him. He would have to do this delicately.

Phillip had reached the REM stage of sleep, the window that would allow the captain to enter his dreams. The first dream Phillip had began on the shores of nowhere in particular. He was seated on a beach, fairly close to the water's edge, but not enough to get wet.

Each ocean wave grew to maximum height, whitecapped, and crashed upon the water below. Then it withdrew to the ocean, to once again repeat its journey up the shore.

Phillip watched the waves come and go. The captain decided to approach Phillip from his left side, as if he were just taking a leisurely walk along the beach. *Hello,* the captain began. Phillip raised his attention from the ocean to examine the familiar voice.

I've met you before, correct?

You are a bright boy. That is correct. Slowly the captain sat down next to Phillip on the sand, joining in watching the mesmerizing ocean waves. *I must speak to you.*

Thank you for your help. Phillip felt uneasy, wondering why this person approached him with such familiarity. *May I ask one question?*

I will try to answer.

An honest reply and an honest face did not convince Phillip of this man's good intentions. *Who are you?*

I can tell you who I am not. A backward answer did not surprise Phillip, who had yet to receive a straight answer from the voices in his head.

Be patient, I know you are confused. I must tell you beforehand that I can hear your thoughts. When you need me, call me Captain. I am always with you and have been since your conception. I am not the voice you heard in the mess hall; I want to make that fact clear here and now. The captain's voice was fatherly yet forceful.

Phillip experienced a feeling of total comfort throughout his mind and body. He knew he could trust the captain as far as to ask him who this "other" voice belonged to.

It is no secret to you that he wishes you were dead. This statement came as no surprise to Phillip since the other voice had told him, " . . . *if you cannot succeed, you will die, and I will have accomplished my goal.*" It appeared that the captain knew nothing about this, and Phillip wanted to discuss what the voice had said concerning the journey ahead of him.

The first mystery he needed to solve concerned the reasons why he had been ordered to meet the three men.

Phillip awoke refreshed, knowing he must complete the task given to him. The dream he'd experienced filled his memory. He could play it over and over again in his mind, picture perfect, but one aspect of it in particular seemed to haunt him. At a certain point the captain had repeated several times, "*Under no circumstances are you to annoy him or let him know I am within you. I feel he does not know.*"

The most interesting fact of the dream figure he'd encountered was that he had a birthmark in the same spot as Phillip. Philip remembered the captain's face as he showed Phillip the mark in his dream. It was the same size, same location, and the same coloring and texture as Phillip's.

It seemed an idiotic thing to remember, but it put a smile on Phillip's face for the start of his day. He was feeling strong and longed to share his excitement. No. He decided it was better not to say a word to anyone about his "voices." He would be thrown out of the military, guilty or not.

Phillip showered, donned his uniform, and arrived at the mess hall by 0600 hours. The other men straggled in slowly. For once the meal did not consist of the usual fare, but good ol' pancakes and waffles! Phillip knew right away something was not right.

At the entrance to the mess hall, each man was given a complete listing of the day's duty roster. Phillip scanned it carefully, mumbling to himself as he read off each position. The list was in order of superiority. Due to the fact that Talreja and his two followers were the newest arrivals, Phillip saw that they had been assigned to breakfast duty and had been up since 0300 hours. Phillip had no clue as to why they'd prepared the particular type of fare they'd served up.

Someone was behind him, breathing hot air on his neck. Talreja bent to Phillip's ear, whispering, "My friend, I hope you enjoyed your breakfast." He walked away before Phillip could respond.

Phillip began to daydream, thinking of nothing in particular.

Hey! Inside Phillip's head, he heard the captain bellow. How could he respond if he couldn't speak to the voice, Phillip wondered.

I can hear your thoughts, remember? Don't let Talreja overpower you. He may not mean anything by his statement, but, the captain paused dramatically, *you do not know what these beings are capable of.*

Phillip realized he was making faces as he listened to the captain; however, no one around him seemed to be paying him any attention. Across the hall was a window to the kitchen, and he had a clear view of Manel and Lock scrubbing pots. Phillip laughed to himself. Both idiots were peering out the window at him. Watching them banging around the pots and pans, it seemed to him they were born klutzes.

No, they are not clumsy. They are practicing controlling a new body. I believe that if these two are part of an evil entity then they cannot control a good soul even if the body accepts the evil one.

What do you mean by that? Phillip was outraged to think that this was what the captain had done to him. His suspicions grew until the captain spoke again.

Nothing. Actually, I commend myself for thinking of it.

Phillip heard the captain sigh and wondered if he really knew what he was doing. A novice, maybe? No. He must be receiving advice from someone.

The captain continued, ignoring Phillip's accusations. *I do not believe it was for the same reason, although the process of one soul combining with another is similar to what happened to us. I was told that I was to be the soul within you, but as I see it, you have your own soul. Now I am wondering just who is leading whom?*

Maybe we could find out what they are up to if we speak to Talreja, Phillip thought hesitantly, though he was determined not to complete the task. Talreja, he felt, could not be trusted. The captain agreed.

Later on that evening, a long-awaited celebration followed dinner. For some of the men it meant simply a time of rest and relaxation; but for most of them it was a time to get smashed. There were no duties scheduled for the next morning except for those poor souls who were to serve the morning meal.

Phillip had waited several weeks for the gathering. He'd spent too many hours working and thinking or doing absolutely nothing, and too few writing letters to his family.

On the carrier's deck, scattered about, were tables filled with people. The noisy crowd was drinking, laughing, and eating. Phillip arrived an hour late, having come from a meeting with his superiors where they'd discussed the various suspects connected with the downing of this plane. Thinking of the three men he'd been told to meet, Phillip convinced the officials that the best person to head the investigation was himself.

Relax! The word echoed through his mind. Someone poured a drink for him and placed it just beyond his reach. It was Manel. Phillip was hesitant to drink any alcohol, but he decided he was entitled to a few.

Beware!

There it went again. Phillip demanded the bellowing be stopped, and the captain reluctantly obliged. Phillip slowly stood. He was almost a foot taller than Manel, who scurried about spilling beer as he rushed to serve the entire table. Then he disappeared into the crowd. Phillip laughed. Several of the men around him also laughed drunkenly.

Soon after the laughing had died down, Talreja appeared. His face steaming, his eyes piercing the crowd with a deadly stare, he seemed ready to lash out at anyone who said a word. "As you all know, the dance is about to begin," he announced, then he left quietly, knowing his statement was dramatic and effective.

Phillip honestly wanted to relax. When he spied one of the beautiful women who'd boarded the ship earlier, his plans half changed. He was not relaxing, but he sure was planning to get smashed, and more. All twenty-one women, dressed fancifully, mingled with the crowd, aiming to seduce the men with their charming smiles.

Long time for you, Cap'? Phillip teased his "voice."

Quiet! I do not wish to speak of that!

Phillip had guzzled his first beer, thinking to refill his mug many times before the evening ended. He wondered if the alcohol would affect the captain, but as it turned out, the captain remained alert throughout Phillip's drinking spree.

A soft hand on his shoulder suddenly startled Phillip. A woman he'd noticed before was now behind him, wanting him to dance. Phillip forgot about his next refill of beer and guided the woman onto the makeshift dance floor.

As one song ended, another one quickly began. The two continued dancing through the next four songs until Phillip grew thirsty for his next beer. When they returned to the table, he noticed his mug had been filled, so he guzzled it down. Thinking the woman might be thirsty as well, Phillip signaled Manel. The man came over reluctantly and gave the woman a glass of wine.

Her name, she claimed, was Ashina. A professional dancer, she was light on her feet and followed Phillip's lead with ease. They began to talk as they joined the others at the table, ignoring the not well hidden smiles and jibes when Phillip held her hand in his lap.

Ashina was surprisingly comfortable, being that she was the only female at his table. Her long red hair was neatly braided to one side, appearing to be short, depending on which side she was seen from.

"You dance quite well, sir." Ashina blushed as she paid Phillip the compliment.

"Thank you. I owe it to my mother. How long have you been on tour with your group?"

Ashina was deep in thought, almost hesitating to answer. "I've been traveling throughout the States with another group, but they recently canceled their tour. I joined this tour a few weeks ago. The girls seem to be nice, but I feel I have more experience in pleasing, if you know what I mean."

Phillip knew exactly what she meant, but he decided to keep his reaction to himself. The captain commended Phillip on his self-control, for he did not trust the woman. Phillip felt the need to change the subject fast before alcohol overcame his better judgment. "How did you learn to dance so well?" he asked.

Ashina hesitated again as if she was listening to her answer before the words left her mouth. "I began dancing when I was a little girl. My parents were well-known dancers, and they felt that I had their gift. I was an only child so it was difficult to refuse their generosity when they wanted to pay for my lessons."

She hesitated again, and a distant look, which made Phillip uneasy, came into her eyes. Every time he asked a question, she would seem to drift off then come back with a full, detailed answer. Ashina was very persistent in her desire to take Phillip away from the dance so she could "please him." "You are still holding my hand. Do you like me?"

Phillip regarded her question with care, hoping he could answer her honestly without leading her on. "You're a beautiful woman. Any man here would enjoy your company." He hesitated, watching her reaction. "Aren't you supposed to mingle?"

"Yes, but I prefer to be by your side for now." There was no hesitation. It was as if she knew the answer without having to look inside herself for a response.

Phillip could not figure this woman out, but he was intrigued and he decided that by the end of the evening, he would know exactly who Ashina was.

Ashina suddenly withdrew her hand from Phillip's grasp and asked the man sitting next to her to dance. After they left the table, the captain was more than impatient to speak to Phillip about her.

I do not trust this woman. There is something about her that I just don't like. Did you see how fast she disappeared when you began to wonder who she was? He spoke rapidly, but Phillip understood the captain's concern.

She can't hear me think; only you can.

Don't be too sure of that. Her eyes are a dead giveaway.

There was a certain tension between the captain and Phillip, a feeling neither of them could explain. Both were baffled by Ashina's reaction, but as long as Phillip kept his composure he could not be persuaded to do anything he did not wish. Losing interest in Ashina, he decided to slam down three more beers.

By the time Ashina returned to his table, Phillip was well on his way to the drunken state he had planned to reach. Ashina thought it best to try again for his company, but the captain began speaking for Phillip.

"What do you want with me, miss?"

Taken aback by the forceful question, Ashina hesitated longer than ever before she responded. She glanced around the table to be sure no one was listening and leaned toward Phillip to express her so-called "true" feelings. "I desire you. Isn't that enough?" She was frustrated, but continued to try to convince Phillip to join her alone away from the crowded deck.

"Why do you want me when there are hundreds of other men on this ship?"

Ashina was again disturbed by his question, but she answered, hesitating before her reply. "Why wouldn't I desire you? You are the most handsome man aboard. Besides, I noticed you staring at me when I arrived."

She thought she had convinced him with her answer, but again, another question followed.

"All the men were staring at your group. Why did you choose to be with me?"

The captain was pleased with himself for thinking of such intelligent questions. Phillip had completely blacked out, so the captain had full control of his body and mind. He was curious to find out exactly what this woman wanted, and he decided to give in to her. "Would you like to have a tour of the ship?" he asked.

"Yes! Oh, my!" Her excitement gave her away. She surely wanted to be alone with Phillip. But why?

"I've always wanted to see what the insides of a ship looked like." She hesitated again with her blank look then continued. "Oh, I mean *this* ship. Of course I have seen others on my previous tours."

There! Mistake number one. The woman was clearly after something and the captain thought he would find out soon.

The captain took her hand as they rose from the table and led her to the main bunker entrance. She stopped before the door and asked if they could "stroll" along the deck so she could see the other end of the ship. They were completely alone when they reached the opposite deck.

Ashina took the tie out of her braid to release her hair to the wind. It was beautiful as it swayed in the breeze, sometimes hitting her face, sometimes flowing behind her. "So, does this excite you?" she asked as she walked beside him, her hands drifting around his waist. It was a soothing massage, yet he was wary of the pressure. Suddenly, without any notice, Ashina pushed him forward, apparently hoping he would fall overboard with no one the wiser. The captain grabbed onto a small hand rail as Phillip's body was forced over the rail. He yelled to her to help him, but instead she began pounding on his hand to make him let go his hold on the ship.

The captain was feeling Phillip's drunken weariness as he hung onto the rail, not realizing that he himself could find the energy to override Phillip's present state with his own strength.

Ashina laughed and continued to pound on his hand. "Die, bastard, die!" she screamed.

The captain finally realized he could command his own strength. He punched Ashina with his free hand. She fell backward, giving him enough time to grip a higher hand bar and hoist himself back on deck. Ashina was still flat on her back when the captain planted both feet by her side. She had hit her head on the deck as she had fallen.

The captain muttered a few four-letter words as he carried the unconscious woman back to the gathering. The ship's doctor was rushed to her side, and directed the captain to the medical room. Many of the girls were confused as to who Ashina was. No one in her group could identify her. Several questions were directed at Phillip, demanding answers as to Ashina's condition.

The captain knew Phillip was still out. "The bitch tried to push me overboard!" he exclaimed. "I was able to knock her out and save myself. Unfortunately, she hit her head on the way down."

That was all they needed to hear. Phillip was a trustworthy man, and they took his word as truth.

"An investigation will be started tomorrow. For now, you men get back to the gathering and forget this happened." The doctor pushed everyone out of the room and slammed the door.

The next morning proved to be more confusing than the previous night. The doctor swore he had restrained Ashina to the cot, but someone released her and she was nowhere to be found on board ship. Due to the previous day's accident, the group of girls were picked up by their tour ship later in the afternoon. A census was taken by the tour director and all the girls were accounted for.

"I swear to you that I have gone over my list several times and I am not missing a single woman!" the tour director bellowed through the radio in frustration, not knowing who Ashina was and not caring. The tour ship was quickly on its way to its next stop.

Phillip meanwhile had the worst hangover of his life as he had not consumed that much alcohol in several years. The captain explained to him what had happened the previous night, and Phillip thanked him several times for saving his life once again. It would be a long time before Phillip would drink again. Talreja, Manel, and Lock never approached Phillip that day.

CHAPTER 7

Phillip had not heard from Talreja in several years. The last time he had spotted him was at the ship's port, where they had docked after completing their surveillance mission. Phillip had been confused, but he was not about to ask Talreja what his assignment had been. Until now.

As far as the military was concerned, whoever had sabotaged Phillip's plane had not been caught. Phillip himself had entered politics after he was discharged, with honors, from the military. The economy was in a shambles, which prompted Phillip to secure a seat as governor. At first he'd been hesitant, but his friends had convinced him that he was the best for the job. He'd served several years, solving problems that previous governors had been unable to solve. He had completed a new budget, which would please not only the residents of the state, but all who contributed to taxes around the country. This new type of budget was incorporated throughout the country and secured the economy. The large deficit was not completely cured, but the new budget allowed the states and their people more buying power than ever before. As was appropriate, the more people spent and put back into the economy, the better the economy was.

The captain, and also Phillip's parents, were proud of him, not only because of his success, but because of his complete honesty in the way he ran his office. No one had ever thought there could be an honest politician. But Phillip never promised anything he could not deliver.

Phillip kept in the back of his mind the fact that he still had some kind of duty to do or he would die. Of course, bad things may become dormant, but they eventually come around again. This time Phillip was prepared. The voice came again, not while he was awake, but in his dreams.

For several years Phillip had been waking up, screaming, from nightmares, not knowing what or who was haunting him. Even the captain was completely blocked off from Phillip's nightmares and was unable to answer his questions.

Hypnotism proved to be a partial success. Although he was relieved to find out what was disturbing him, Phillip was afraid for his life as well as for others around him. "Satan," as he referred to him, was back again.

One nightmare had sent Phillip flying, face first, into the backboard of his bed. He had smashed his face, breaking a tooth and giving himself a huge black eye. His wife had to wake him even after he had collided with the wooden backboard. If she had not brought him to consciousness, he would have swallowed the fragment of tooth that had broken off. He felt no pain until the next morning. It was the last time he put up with his nightmares; afterward he began seeing a hypnotist.

Fifty sessions had gone by before the doctor gave up. There were certain things Phillip had said while under hypnosis that the doctor knew he must never repeat. Phillip knew that "Satan" had a part in all this. He knew that Ashina had failed in her task. He also knew that there would certainly be more mischief done to him, but he never thought his dreams could affect him so much. The captain had told Phillip, "He cannot enter your dreams." But as it had turned out, he did and this continued to be a mystery to the captain as well as to Phillip.

"Satan" had been carefully following Phillip's political career. Up to now, Phillip had never done any harm to anyone, and he did not realize that "Satan" had other plans for him.

Phillip won his first presidential election! The celebration party, planned by Felicia, was a success, of course. She was an excellent wife, not only for her faithfulness and her ability to put up with Phillip's long working hours, but also because she could manage his affairs. As a recipient of a Ph.D. in psychology, she was able to guide Phillip through many difficult television interviews and hordes of reporters with their numerous questions. The cause of his success, though, was his honesty. Above all, Phillip was honest!

Felicia was fifteen years younger than Phillip. The age difference had never bothered either them or their supporters, but they had decided to wait until after the inauguration to have children. There had been too much pressure on them during Phillip's recent campaign to even consider the idea.

The captain had never revealed himself to Felicia. He had a way of hiding within Phillip so that the couple could enjoy each other without Phillip being concerned about a "listener" or third party. Phillip had met Felicia during his first year as governor. She was, and continued to be, extremely independent and full of energy. Her features were different than any woman Phillip had ever dated. He usually chose women with long, black hair and with a delicate build. Felicia had long, strawberry-tinted blond hair. Her build was delicate; yet she was physically and mentally strong. She had an incredible figure, which Phillip always complimented her on. She was beautiful, intelligent, strong, and very funny. As his best friend and "pal," she loved him very much.

There was only one secret Phillip kept from her: the voices he heard. He did not want to put her in jeopardy by telling her that he was lucky to be alive and that he had been ordered to complete some mission which even he knew nothing of. The captain agreed and justified Phillip's decision. If Felicia knew, she would be killed as well if he did not succeed.

It was early spring, long after the inauguration, when Phillip heard "Satan" again. This time he was fully awake and sitting at his desk.

You have done well, my boy. "Satan's" voice was deeper, yet it was the same voice Phillip had heard many years ago.

Will you stop calling me "boy"? I've grown out of that. Phillip was playing with "Satan" to determine what kind of a reaction he would receive. He expected and received the same response.

"My boy?" Do those words really bother you? Tsk, tsk, tsk. I do apologize for my behavior.

Phillip imagined "Satan" was being sarcastic, but amazingly enough, he was never called "boy" again.

It is time you met with Talreja, the voice continued. *He has worked for you for several years. He will knock on your door in one hour.*

That was the last Phillip heard "Satan" say before Talreja was knocking on his door. Where had the time gone? The captain assured him that he had fallen asleep out of pure exhaustion. There had been no foul play during the missing hour.

Phillip heard the knocking become louder and faster. Talreja was persistent. But when he opened the door, a woman with long, black hair and a delicate figure stood before him.

"Talreja?" Phillip could not believe his eyes. Talreja was, or used to be, male, but now. . . .

"Don't be alarmed. The old Talreja failed his mission. He was disposed of. I am nicer than he." She entered the room.

"Nice? How can you be nice when you have evil inside

you?" Phillip was still in shock to see a woman at his door, but he kept his composure, hoping to discover her mission. "Why are you here? What must I do to get rid of all of you?"

"You cannot get rid of us. We are always here. We have been since time began. Now enough of the chit-chat." She paused, not as Ashina had, but a thoughtful pause. "As I see it, the first thing you must do is abolish all types of abortion. There is to be another world war, but that is not scheduled for your lifetime. Many humans die."

"To me that sounds good. How can you do good when you are pure evil?" Phillip was confused but he knew the captain was listening intently, though he was keeping silent for some unknown reason.

"Ah, it will come clear to you in the end. The second task you must do is to abolish taxes." She smiled, knowing he was absolutely confused.

"That is also good in a way. What is your purpose?"

"Stop asking questions and let me continue. Your problem is that you do not listen! Now, listen!" She was very demanding, motherly, yet evil. "The third task you must accomplish is to abolish all weapons that are able to travel long distances and cause major damage." She smiled again.

Phillip was even more confused than before she'd knocked on his door. "You realize these type of decisions must be addressed to Congress, don't you?" He thought he had her stumped, but he did not.

"Yes. We took care of that many years ago. Where do you think Manel and Lock have been?" She smiled again, except this time she continued without waiting for an answer. "Your fourth and final mission is to abolish bigotry within this country."

"This is still confusing me, and I know you are well aware of it. Why do you want me to do these things?"

"You know I cannot answer you. Why do you persist?"

She waited for his response, then continued as if he had taken too long. "Do these tasks and I will return when they are completed."

"How do you expect me to do all of this? How long do I have?"

"There is no time limit, but the faster you complete these first four tasks, the better for you, your wife, and children." That last statement frightened Phillip. He knew he had to act fast.

The first two tasks were completed within his first year in office. His followers rejoiced as did the Pro-Life believers. Others were not as enthused with the outcome of their president's decision.

Abolish taxes? Phillip had thought long and hard on this one. He decided to declare that persons earning less than $25,000 a year were exempt from taxes. It was agreed that this task was complete.

The last two tasks were the most difficult. Even Manel and Lock had several problems convincing Congress to abolish all long-range weapons, but the task of abolishing bigotry was the most difficult task the four men had encountered.

During these years Phillip and Felicia had had a boy, named David, and a girl, named Dana, the elder of the two. Phillip was lost in his work at times, but he always found time for his family.

Bigotry had existed for thousands of years. Phillip had been the only one out of the four to come up with an idea. Most of the bigoted people had died during the past century, but it still existed among a select few. At this time, there were at least three groups of people left who were not in agreement with this new "fad," as they had called it.

Phillip suggested bringing these three groups of people together by having them work together on a daily basis.

Manel and Lock were assigned to pass certain laws through Congress, which made these "work forces" economically necessary. Each group had their own specific talents, which only they could contribute to reach a final bonding.

The "work," as Phillip called it, was based on education. It was decided that each school must teach young children about different heritages. It was difficult for an American to teach American children about Africa, Russia, South America, India, Venice, Australia, Japan, and even the Philippines. They may have been doctors in their field, but they could not penetrate the children's minds as well as a native of the land in which they were studying.

The children of each class consisted of all kinds of religions, races, and heritages. With the growth of the economy and the baby boom, there were thousands of classes held throughout the country every day. Therefore, since there were thousands of classes, there was a need for hundreds of teachers. Each set of three teachers were able to permanently impress upon the children's minds that there are many ways of doing things to achieve the same result.

It had taken Phillip's entire term to complete this task. He recalled having grown up in all-white schools, with all-white teachers and all-white ways. Now children were developing a higher intelligence, knowing that whatever way they chose to accomplish a goal, it was right even though different from someone else's view.

The strangest thing that developed from this experiment was that there was no need to define people by their heritage; it simply did not exist. Many of these students had taken class trips, funded by the government, to different countries on a regular basis. The children were fascinated by the way their individual ancestors had developed throughout their several thousand years of existence.

Phillip was proud of himself and of his country for

succeeding in such a different atmosphere than that in which he had grown up. The final test, which would complete his goal, was to determine if there were any long-term effects. This seemed to satisfy Talreja when she returned to Phillip the day after he won the next election."You have done well. I am proud of all of you." Periodically, Talreja had assisted the three men in their tasks, but she had never directly interfered. "Now, with the three of you present, he may speak."

She waited for silence as the three men sat in Phillip's office, the door locked, all connections to the room blocked.

My friends. You have done well. Thank you, Talreja, for your assistance.

There was a short pause and suddenly the three men heard a piercing scream as Talreja vanished from their sight. Not only Phillip, but Manel and Lock, as stupid as they were, became wary. They had no idea what had become of Talreja. *Now, as for you two,* Manel and Lock held their breath and waited for "Satan" to continue, *go back to your homes, I will call on you when you are needed next.* The two men ran from the room faster than Phillip had ever thought possible.

For fifty years I have waited. For fifty years I have planned. Now, since you have completed your tasks, I must leave, but I will return. You will know when the time is near.

Phillip was confused again. The captain was still with him, guiding him, helping him and his family. Neither knew what these four tasks would mean for his future. What kind of goal did this evil voice have in mind?

CHAPTER 8

By the end of Phillip's third term, there were several problems, among them the fact that the country was overcrowded. No one could have predicted this outcome since during the past eight years the country had developed so well.

What went wrong? Phillip asked the captain, needing support.

I do not know. Someone must have interfered. How, I do not know.

Phillip's patience was growing thin. The following day, halfway through his fourth year as president, a war developed between two rich and well-developed countries. It was up to Phillip to decide upon a course of intervention. But how? His country was economically in danger, although there were still ways of increasing income. How could he help these two countries end the fighting?

Dana and David came home from high school with several of their friends. They all piled into Phillip's office with Felicia's approval.

"Dad? We have a proposal for you." Dana was a strong-minded little lady, stronger than Phillip ever dreamed she could be.

"To what do I owe this pleasure?" He looked around the room at the other teenagers, wondering what they were up to now.

"Sir, if I may?" David always respected his father's

status by calling him "sir" whenever he wanted to talk about business. "We've drawn up a plan to help you stop the war. Would you like to see it?"

"I'd be happy to, David, but I see this plan you have is almost a thousand pages long. Can you give me the main idea in your own words?"

"Oh, the whole thing is not the plan. It's filled with signatures from kids around the world. See?" David flipped through the pages, showing his father the signatures of many children.

"Impressive. Now tell me your idea." Phillip was proud of his children for trying to help, and he gave them his full attention for the next five hours. The captain listened in as well.

"The first thing we have to do is get each of these children over to the war zone. Directly between the lines."

"What?" Phillip was shocked to think that his children would jeopardize not only their own lives, but others' lives as well.

"Wait, you haven't heard the whole thing. We know our country is packed with people and money seems to be scarce, but I think we can do it with the help of the rest of the world." David paused, trying to contain his excitement. "With the help of all the children who endorsed these pages, we can force the two sides into signing a peace treaty. Believe me, Dad, or sir, we're not alone in this idea."

The captain became preoccupied, so much so that Phillip was unable to get his attention. Philip regarded his son with concern. "You do realize that I cannot make this decision on my own?"

"Yes, but with your support, we may have a chance." David was an overly anxious young man, constantly interrupting people only because he would lose his train of thought. "Please give us the benefit of your support. We'll take it to Congress ourselves."

Dana and David continued to argue with their father for several hours, giving him specific details on how, why, and when. Phillip decided to give in, knowing that Congress would never approve. Still he was proud of his children for taking on such a difficult task.

The war continued while Congress debated what to do for several months. Manel and Lock supported the children's idea and surprisingly received support from every member of Congress. Phillip was in shock when he was notified of the decision. He decided to veto the decision but was overruled. His children and thousands of others were beginning plans on their departure.

The leaders of each side of the war agreed to a cease-fire so that the children could be safely transported to the front lines. The departure date was set. Phillip had only two weeks to stop them.

The voice came again to Phillip. *Do not stop your children's mission. You will regret it.*

Why do you support this action? What is your goal? You've already begun to destroy my country. Why do you insist upon placing the children in such danger?

You must realize that only the children can stop this war. You have no weapons and no money to do it yourself.

Phillip needed the captain desperately. He sought him in his mind, but could get no response. *This war was started due to your interference. If you had not made my country so weak, we could have stopped them before the fighting began,* Phillip thought.

He called again for the captain and received a *wait a minute* response. At least the captain was still there, but Phillip needed advice immediately. For some reason Phillip could not explain, the "Satan" voice never heard him call for the captain, although "Satan" claimed that he could hear Phillip's thoughts.

I am in another part of your brain that he cannot penetrate. Don't worry. I'll be right there. I'm busy at the moment. The captain left Phillip again.

"Satan" was strangely calm, as if he had planned for the war to begin only for his own purposes. *You must not interfere with your children's initiative. You should be proud of them and not stop them!*

I am proud, but I must stop this insanity. The war was started over an argument about resources, meaning that it has nothing to do with those children. The only children I see are the leaders of the two countries!

Calm down. There is no need to get upset. I need those children over there. It is not necessary for you to know why.

Not necessary? You've already lied to me. You said there would be no more wars in my lifetime! Phillip was outraged, not only because of his strong commitment to stop the transport, but because the captain was not with him. *These are my children! Of course I have the right to get upset!*

The captain returned to Phillip, interrupting any thought he was about to blurt out. *Do not let your children go. I have found out something very interesting. If you are capable, get rid of him. We need to talk.*

Phillip had no control over "Satan," but he came up with an idea to temporarily send him away. *All right. I won't stop them,* he lied. In his mind he thought of this as the truth effectively enough to satisfy "Satan."

Good. Remember, I will be watching you. "Satan" went away, relieving Phillip of his tension.

Now that he is gone, I must enter your dream. You must fall asleep, the captain said.

Why can't we discuss this now? Phillip was confused, but he backed down and prepared himself to sleep.

When Phillip reached REM sleep, he opened his eyes in his dream and saw the captain pacing along the shoreline. *I must show you something. That is why I needed you here and not awake.* The captain paused to pick up a seashell, rubbed it a few times, and skipped it across the waves. *You must not let your children go. I have been quite busy discussing this matter among others.*

What others? Who else is in my mind? Phillip could not believe that there was anyone else within him. How many could fit?

You do not need to know to whom I have spoken, but you must know the possible outcome of your children's mission.

How can you tell the future? Phillip asked the captain more out of his own curiosity than anything else.

I cannot predict the future, but someone else knows why your children have been prompted to do what they have done so far. How do you think Congress was persuaded? Manel and Lock are not real people as you see them. They were real until "he" got a hold of them.

I figured as much. How can you show me the outcome of their mission? As soon as he stopped talking, the shoreline faded into the front lines of the war. Several soldiers with machine guns were running toward an enemy camp, planning to storm it with grenades and take over. The next fade-in brought a ceasefire. All Phillip could see in the sky were multiple transport planes circling the area, landing on the makeshift runways one by one. As the planes settled, their doors opened, and more than three hundred children emerged from each plane.

The scene faded again; this time Phillip recognized the leaders of each side, who were now, seating themselves on the border among the children. The scene faded again. Phillip's heart pounded within him when he saw the next scene. The long line of people had been murdered and were being prepared for burial directly on the border. Phillip raced through the lines; Dana and David were nowhere to be found.

Where are my children? he shouted to the soldiers digging the graves. No one answered. The scene faded to the shoreline once again. As Phillip stood in the water, he began to cry. The captain stood silently behind him, allowing Phillip the moment of mourning he needed. He mourned more for the thousands of children than for his own grief. *Why did you show me this?* He was confused, disturbed, and tired.

It is not known what will happen to Dana and David, but it is definite that all of those children will die. The war will end, not because the border resources dispute was settled, but because it will be considered a sacred burial place, thereby denying both countries access to these resources.

When Phillip woke, he found himself dripping in his own perspiration. He was now more determined than ever to stop the transport.

CHAPTER 9

Phillip's next presidential campaign was successful. He won and would continue in office for four more years. He had been able to stop the transport of the children, disgusting "Satan," by convincing the several countries involved not to send the delegated children to the war. The transport had been declared economically and humanly damaging to each country. His children were disappointed, but they quickly forgave him, for he was their father and their friend. Above all, they trusted him.

The day began with a bright warm sunrise. A soft breeze floated through the trees. Phillip had planned to take Felicia and the children to an immense ranch to ride the horses, providing something of a quiet vacation for his family. Of course, they were all closely guarded, but they were able to enjoy each other's company away from the hustle and bustle of Phillip's responsibilities.

The war had ended shortly after his inauguration. He was relieved to receive the news, but he continued to be concerned about "Satan's" threats regarding his interference with the transport.

Phillip and his family enjoyed the first week of their vacation, dining under the trees and riding the horses through the countryside.

On the eighth day, disaster struck. A new horse had been delivered to the barn that morning. It was said to be a "gift" for the family to enjoy. Felicia had completed her morning chores and was tempted to ride the newest addition. The stable boy provided her with a saddle and sent her off on her own into the field. Phillip and the children watched from the porch, keeping a close eye on her, as did one of the body-guards who followed close behind her. The bodyguards always kept their distance from the family so as to not suffocate them with their attention, but not so far away that they could not provide protection if needed.

Felicia's horse suddenly reared up on its hind legs, throwing her to the ground. As if suddenly disturbed, it turned on Felicia and began trampling her as she crawled off in panic, trying to reach safety. The bodyguard jumped from his still-moving horse to go to Felicia's aid but it was too late. Her skull had been completely smashed by the force of the horse's hooves.

The horse was immediately shot after Felicia's body was carefully placed on the porch, her head covered with blood, her lifeless body surrounded by her grieving husband and children. They had seen the torment their mother suffered.

Felicia was buried the next day. The country mourned for the death of the first lady. Not one person in the country had a dry face. Phillip and the children were severely depressed as the weeks passed by. Several doctors were assigned to each of them for counseling and consolation.

"Satan" came back to Phillip one month after his wife's demise. *I told you not to interfere!* His voice was deeper now, impatience growing within him.

Why have you taken the dearest thing to my heart?

That's just it! I warned you! "Satan" was becoming more evil than ever. This may have been the result of his defeat, but Phillip would never know. He vowed the evil entity would pay for having taken his beloved wife away from him.

I have another task for you. This time, do it or your children die too! the voice commanded.

Phillip had no choice. He had already lost his wife; he did not want to lose his children as well. The captain agreed but told Phillip to decide on his actions after the task was stated. *State your needs!* Phillip raised his voice in fury, hoping to intimidate "Satan," but he was unsuccessful.

I cannot be intimidated. His voice was calm, replying to Phillip's thoughts once again. *Your task is a simple one.* He paused, waiting for a response from Phillip. No response followed; Phillip did not want to back down or give away his fear of evil.

I no longer need you in politics. You must step down.

Phillip's mouth dropped. He was stunned by the request and immediately refused.

Then your children must die! "Satan" was determined to be successful in his request. Phillip was completely stumped. He had to step down; he must save his children.

Take me instead! Phillip thought he could sacrifice himself for his children. The captain screamed, *No!*

Well, well, well, you are so valiant, aren't you? You would complete my goal for me? I thank you!

No! Wait! I will step down! Phillip granted "Satan" his wish, not only to save his children from harm, but because they had already lost their mother and they did not need to grieve for him as well.

The news spread rapidly. The excuse Phillip gave for his decision was the collapsed economy. There were no other reasons he could think of.

The unexpected event caused mass hysteria throughout the country. Phillip's resignation was denied. The economy had been improving each month and no one believed his excuse. He was confused once again. What should he do? He had tried to do what "Satan" had told him, but he'd been unsuccessful. It was several weeks before "Satan" returned.

You have failed! I will return with another task for you. Be patient. As suddenly as it had come, the presence disappeared.

Phillip needed the captain more than ever.

I'm here.

What do I do? Be patient? Patient for what? My whole life has been controlled by him! When will it stop?

I have been unable to discover the reason why he wants you destroyed. There is, however, one thing that only you can do that will annoy him. The captain paused, hesitating to tell Phillip what he needed to hear.

In exactly two months, there will be a conference scheduled involving every world leader. The objective of this meeting will be how to save the Earth. You, Phillip, will be the one to lead the conference.

There it was, as clear as anything Phillip had ever heard in his entire life. He could not figure out why "Satan" needed the earth to be destroyed, but he knew now why his life had been in danger since his birth. The first four tasks he had been given had sounded good at the time, but he concluded that each task had been part of "Satan's" plan to destroy him.

By abolishing abortions, the country would become overcrowded. By abolishing taxes for lower income households, the government would surely lose the use of funds for certain city-wide projects. By abolishing all destructive weapons, it would leave the country defenseless against its enemies. Abolishing bigotry, however, was incomparable to the rest. Phillip did not know how this last task had weaved its way into "Satan's" plans. With bigotry abolished, everyone worked and lived peacefully among each other.

The tasks completed had not all been successful according to "Satan's" plans. Abortion was abolished, but since the lower classes were able to spend more money on health care, there was an explosion in the market for birth control. The stock exchange had gone through the roof. The abolishment of long-range weapons had enabled the government to spend money on the economy, which eventually grew, and nearly recovered to the point where it had been before Phillip served his first term.

The abolishment of bigotry made the younger children more intent on saving the world to make it a better place for their children. They were properly educated about the world's problems and began inventing ways of preserving the environment.

Phillip began his worldwide campaign by interviewing every leader to convince them to attend the conference he planned to have. Many leaders were hesitant but eventually decided to attend.

The conference was due to take place the following month. All of the details concerning living arrangements and meals had been attended to, and the largest conference building in the world was reserved. Phillip's ratings as president skyrocketed during this time period. He had 90 percent of the population's support, and it continued to grow. Even citizens who had never before voted took advantage of a preliminary poll.

The press was extremely active, gathering information and interviewing all politicians. Things were going well for Phillip until the final two weeks before the conference. The disasters were supposedly "natural" but only one entity was able to create these menaces.

Due to the hot, dry summer weather and help from "Satan's" minions placed throughout the country, several forest fires had broken out, destroying thousands of acres. There were more earthquakes reported within this two-week period than there had been in the past hundred years, and several cities were destroyed. Many people died in fires, earthquakes and, surprisingly, in car and rail accidents, while strange pockets of wind would send planes hurtling to the ground.

These disasters did not stop Phillip from continuing his plans for the upcoming conference. "Satan" threatened to kill Phillip's children again, but the captain was able to protect them. Phillip had been told, reluctantly, that the captain could give his children "guardians."

This was all that Phillip was told, for the captain had no right to reveal to whom he was connected. Even the captain did not know exactly who it was, but he was certain that these guardians could successfully protect Dana and David. It was unfortunate that the captain had been unaware of this capability before the time of Felicia's death. Phillip thought of her every day, and his memories gave him the strength to fight for the success of the conference.

The so-called natural disasters continued, killing many people along the way. The world was in turmoil, but the conference was still due to take place. Many leaders were hesitant to leave their homelands while these "natural" disasters were occurring, but Phillip was able to persuade them that if they attended the meeting, the disasters would end.

There was still no word from his life-long enemy. The only bad news he received that he had not been expecting was that of the death of his parents. They had lived a full life, which Phillip was thankful for. It had been a terrible rainy day for their joint funeral, but at least Phillip knew that his parents had died together, hopefully of natural causes. It seemed pure coincidence that they had died at the same time in their sleep. Phillip had no proof that "Satan" had anything to do with it, but it would bother him for the rest of his life. Not knowing was the worst.

CHAPTER 10

It seemed to Phillip that the past two days had been too quiet; there had been no natural disasters, no news at all. He began his day, as he had every day since Felicia had died, by lighting a single candle in the bedroom. He prayed for her and for his children, who he hoped were safe. He missed Felicia fiercely. He knew he would never remarry. He did not want to even meet another woman. In Phillip's eyes, no woman in the world could measure up to Felicia.

As Phillip finished his prayer, there was a soft knock at his door. Dana had come to remind him that it was time for them to board the private jet. She knew what her father did every morning and did not wish to disturb him, though she knew that this day was important to all of them.

It had taken two hours to fly to the conference. All the last-minute details were discussed and several documents required Phillip's signature. Dana and David always traveled in their own personal section of the jet. Running through their minds during the flight was the question of whether or not the jet would stay aloft. They landed safely hours later, and prepared for the work ahead of them.

Bodyguards surrounded Phillip, Dana, and David as they exited the plane. There were countless numbers of reporters and general on-lookers waiting beyond the ribboned lines for a glimpse or picture of their president and his family. Phillip had always given the reporters his attention, but this particular day was too important for him to be bombarded with questions. There would be time enough afterwards.

They were rushed throughout the airport, still followed closely by their bodyguards. Limousines waited to take them to the Ambassador Hotel, which was completely booked for the pending conference. Only the leaders and their families were allowed through the front doors of the hotel. Bellhops rushed from each car into the hotel, transporting the mass of luggage to each room.

Several leaders had gathered together in the lobby to discuss their ideas, only to discover that their views on how to save the environment were very different. The noise level in the hotel was almost unbearable. The wives and children were sent directly to their respective rooms, more for their safety than comfort. For some, it had been a long trip to the conference. Many had children who had slept during their flights and were now raring to go. Their combined energy level was most irritating to the tired parents who accompanied them.

The hotel had two thousand rooms, five immense conference rooms and four separate dining rooms that were prepared to serve several different types of food according to each country's preference. One conference room had been specifically set up for the younger and older children. The hotel manager had been so pleased to have her establishment responsible for hosting the conference that she had ordered several types of playground equipment, video games, board games, puzzles, and even a library for the teenagers.

Dana and David had no interest in the children's events so they decided to join the wives in the closed circuit room, where they could watch and listen to the historical conference as it happened. The opening ceremony was scheduled to begin after lunch was served, providing the leaders with quality time with their families before they were due in the conference.

Phillip requested that Dana and David join him in the dining hall that served Oriental food, making them try several different dishes not served at home. Even though they had traveled the world while they attended school, it was Oriental food they had always been unwilling to try. Phillip had always made sure that his children were well-educated, not only in their regular studies, but also in the daily life of various cultures.

Along one wall of the dining hall were several tables filled with all types of Oriental dishes, most of which were Japanese, Chinese, and Philippine. Dana and David were most interested in the Japanese sushi. Phillip guided them through each platter set on the buffet tables, describing each dish, first in Japanese and then translating the name into English.

Dana chose a piece of fish placed on a small roll of rice. "Dad, what's this smelly green stuff?" She picked the slice of fish off of the rice to find a green substance spread over the top.

"Oh, that's *wausabi*. It tastes like horseradish, but it's hotter so be careful." Phillip warned her, not wanting her to eat a clump of it in one bite, which would surely clear her sinuses!

"What are these?" David asked as he pointed to a tray filled with sushi.

Phillip described each type of fish and what it tasted like. "This is called *maguro*, which is tuna. If it smells fishy, don't eat it."

"That doesn't make sense!" David roared as he placed five pieces on his plate.

"Well, if it smells fishy it's bad fish or it has been in the air too long. I think the maguro would be the best thing to start out with."

Phillip was bombarded with, "What's this?" and "Yuck! What's that?" So he continued his lecture on all the sushi spread out on the table. "This is *kanikama*, which is crab meat. This is called *shime saba*, which is mackerel. This one you should know." He paused as he made Dana guess the type of fish he held in his hand.

"Is it flounder?" Dana tried hard but it was difficult to decipher what type of fish it was without seeing the whole thing.

"This is *shake*, which is salmon. It's very good! Put a few on your plate. If you don't like it; I'll eat it!"

"Oh, Dad, you just want more for yourself! Look at your plate already!" Phillip's plate was crowded with sushi that some pieces appeared to be close to hitting the floor. David laughed at his father, knowing he had a huge appetite.

Phillip continued his "fish" lesson. "This is *irame*, Dana. It's fluke, or flounder, whatever you want to call it. This funny-looking thing is called *ikura*, which is salmon roe, fish eggs."

"Oh, yuck! They even serve fish eggs?" David would have nothing to do with that!

"This is *unagi*, fresh eel. *Hamachi* is yellow tail. *Tai* is red snapper. *Uni* is sea urchin . . . " Phillip paused as he heard Dana gasp. "What's wrong?"

"It's moving!" She almost dropped her plate as she watched the sea urchin wobble.

"It's alive. You may not want to try that." Phillip could hardly contain his laughter.

"You'd better believe that!" Dana moved to the next platter faster than David and Phillip could follow.

"This is *tako* which is octopus. It's tough but it tastes

good. Now, this is *ebi*, which is shrimp. It's cooked so you'll enjoy that. These are *kaibashira*, which are scallops. They're not alive, although they are often eaten while they're still moving." Phillip waited until the "yucks!" subsided from both children. "This is *ika*, which is squid. You might like that too."

The next table consisted of several types of chicken and pork. "This is chicken *katsu*; it's boneless chicken breaded and deep fried."

"That's not unusual! It's like what Sara used to make." Sara, their cook at home, always made several simple meals for Dana and David while Phillip was away on business. They always ate with their father when he was home, but burgers and hot dogs were not considered a full meal for Phillip.

The last table was filled with several desserts, consisting of green tea, ginger, and vanilla ice cream. There was also *yokan*, which is red bean cake, almond jelly, and lemon-flavored rice. Their plates were filled with sushi and none of them had the room for dessert, so Dana offered to bring them all something sweet later on.

To Phillip, the time was slow passing. He felt he would be in the dining room forever. As he ate, he thought about his opening speech, which had been prepared several weeks in advance, hoping to remember to add a few more ideas he had pondered over on the jet. Even though his speech would be scrolled in front of him as he stood at the podium, he was nervous as always.

"It's almost time, Dad," Dana reminded him softly so as to not to disturb his thoughts. "Do you still want dessert?"

"No, honey. Go get something for you and your brother. I have some things to take care of before the conference begins." Phillip was positive that he was ready for such an important meeting, but he needed to speak to the captain in private.

As he left the dining room, several bodyguards followed closely behind, except for two who were specifically assigned to protect his children. They became a "feeling" of protection rather than "five men" following him wherever he went. Phillip asked the guards to wait outside his room to give him a moment of privacy. His request was granted, but only after the guards searched the room for anything suspicious. Finally all was clear for him to enter the room alone.

Are you here? Phillip thought. Although he knew that the captain was always there, he requested his presence politely.

You don't need to be nervous. I haven't seen you this way in a long time. The captain was concerned for Phillip and decided it was best to let him guide the conversation.

I know, but this is very important to me and the children as well as the world leaders who are here. Phillip paused, thinking of the leaders he had spoken to earlier, knowing he would receive a denial from some of them. He knew he must make it clear to them all that he was not going to back down on any of the ideas he planned to announce in his speech.

Think of Felicia. When the captain said her name, Phillip felt his heart pound inside him, making him remember that Felicia would be proud of him this day. *She would want to be here if she could. Who knows? Maybe she's listening to you now.*

I'm glad you're with me, my friend. I don't know what I would have done without you all these years. Phillip paused, recalling the time he'd fallen into a pool, almost drowning. The captain had explained to him, when Phillip was older, that his father, Cory, was given the captain's strength to save him. *Are you planning to stay with me for the rest of my life? I'd hate to wake up one day and not hear you answer.*

The captain did not know how to respond to the question. After what seemed to be several minutes, he decided to leave the question unanswered. *I'm here now. Isn't that enough?*

No! Phillip was distraught to think that his friend would possibly leave some day. *Do you know how long or are you as confused as I am?*

Concentrate on your speech. Never mind me at the moment. There are some mysteries in life better left unsolved. He sighed and faded into the depths of Phillip's mind.

Phillip paced several times across the room, stopping once to glance at the clock beside the bed. The conference room would be filled by now, he thought. Soon he would hear a knock at the door, requesting his presence at the meeting. He had been calm during the past few minutes, but his body still jerked when the guards pounded on the door. It was time. He was not nervous, only numb inside, wondering what reaction the crowd would have in response to his speech.

"Mr. President?" Phillip heard the voice behind the door, still not believing it was time to present his long-awaited speech. As he opened the door, Dana and David stood by their assigned guards, smiling at their father, for they were proud of him and what he represented. Loving their father deeply, each vowed to protect him from anyone who meant harm.

Down the hallway, down the elevator, and to the conference they all went, traveling close by Phillip. The group paused before the two large doors while Phillip kissed his children for luck. They could hear the crowd inside the hall cheer and jeer as the man at the podium announced the entrance of the president.

The two doors opened simultaneously, releasing an onslaught of people attempting to shake Phillip's hand as the guards quickly led him to the podium. As soon as the crowd became almost inaudible, Phillip began his long-thought-out speech, surrounded by his loyal guards.

"I come today to bring the world together in the fight against the environmental destruction we have all contributed to." A loud mixture of cheers followed his opening statement, soon dying down enough for Phillip to continue. "The earth is our home. I hope to reach our goal by the end of this conference, thanks to all of those who have traveled across the world to attend this historical gathering . . . " Phillip went on, pausing during each interruption of cheers and clapping, relaying his thoughts and proposing plans to help save the environment.

One proposal in particular received a standing ovation and brought every leader into agreement that if one country purposely destroyed their environment, the result would be the death of the leader responsible. It was a strong proposal, and it was widely accepted by all—except one country that had, in a prior war, destroyed its own environment. Though they had succeeded in destroying their environment, they lost the war as well as many of the soldiers who'd fought honorably for their country.

This one leader sat in silence as the entire audience stood and cheered. When the room fell silent again, Phillip continued keeping an eye on his one enemy, his most hated rival. He was expecting something to happen.

Phillip's closing statement brought the audience to their feet once again. This time the applause was louder than the last. "As my last statement for the opening of this conference, I propose that all leaders here today sign their respective contracts, which will allow their neighboring countries to join in the quest to clean up their environment." Several countries had become severely poor due to the rising costs of fixing their mistakes which destroyed, in one way or another, their home.

As the crowd stood cheering and clapping at all they had heard, a gunshot roared above the noise. A body fell to the ground. No one knew who had been hit or who had pulled the trigger. With all the commotion in the conference hall, Dana and David were unable to see their father. Both children raced toward the door to the hall but were immediately restrained by their guards. Dana tried to explain how important it was for her to be by her father's side if he was hurt, but the guard motioned her to be silent while he listened to someone speaking to him on his headset.

Dana, watching the guard's expression, saw him give her a straight, hard look then glance through the window overlooking the crowd. He completed his questions then turned to Dana, who eagerly awaited an answer.

"The President is fine. No need to worry." The guard immediately raced through the door, ordering his partner to stay with the children and wives.

"Who was shot?" one woman demanded, throwing her arms up in confusion.

"I can't relay that information to you. Please, everyone," he raised his hands to silence the group, "take your seats. I will escort you to your rooms when I receive an order to do so."

The guard was calm, yet he seemed to be worried. Dana looked at David. They each nodded to the other, realizing that one of their father's guards must have been the unlucky recipient of the bullet.

Several hours passed of waiting and listening to silent discussions among the wives before word was received that they would be returned to their rooms. There was still no word on who was shot or even the condition of the person.

Dana asked the guard to take her and her brother to Phillip. Their request was denied, which left them even more concerned. Reluctantly, they gave in and followed the guard to their room.

With the conference brought to an immediate halt, there was little hope that it would continue on this day. "It's not a total loss, David. Don't be such a pessimist. There's always tomorrow."

David was furious with his sister's statement, but he abandoned any thought of an argument. "Why do these things always have to happen? It's not Dad's fault. He wanted to do some good." His hand flew in the air, expressing the support of the other leaders. "I want to know who tried to kill Dad!"

"Don't you dare go out there on your own," she warned him with a glowering stare. "Besides, the guard won't let us through the door anyhow." Dana always obeyed orders, but her brother's curiosity was overpowering her better judgment.

"We could get out of here to see Dad if we really wanted to." David looked around the large room for a connecting door to the next room. To his disappointment, there were no other doors except the one at which the guard was posted.

"Isn't there a laundry chute?" Dana was surprised at herself for suggesting another exit.

"I did find something but it's too small for the two of us."

"It's perfect!" Dana screamed as she opened the release door. There was a dumbwaiter box controlled by pulley ropes.

"Okay, dear sister." David gave Dana a loving glance. He admired his sister in many ways. "Let's ask the guard if he's heard anything. If he doesn't give us an answer, well then, I'll go with you." He began pounding on the door, screaming for the guard.

"What!" The guard threw open the door, almost sucking

the air out of the room. He was tired and worried about the other guard, but he tried to calm down for the president's family.

"Sorry, sir. I guess I was just concerned for my father. Have you heard anything yet? Who was shot? When are we getting out of here?"

"Slow down!" he shouted above David's questions. "Now, first of all, I can't let you two roam the hotel by yourselves. Your lives are in as much danger as your father's. I can't take you there either, so don't ask! As for who was shot, you don't need to know." His voice softened as he ended his last statement before locking the door. David could sense that the guard was extremely concerned about his colleague.

"I wonder if that guard who was shot is his friend or something." Dana shot her brother a stern look, as he seemed about to bang on the door again. "Leave him alone. We have a trip to make."

"You're not kidding, are you?" David was surprised but proud of his sister's bravery and quickly whisked her off into the kitchen to begin their prowling.

While David eased himself into the dumbwaiter, Dana decided to stay behind as it was smaller than she had at first thought. She held onto the ropes, a lifeline for David. "I want to see where this goes first, so when I pull on the rope, pull me up."

"You would think this thing would be electrical. So stupid." Dana held onto the ropes as tightly as she could, lowering her brother until she felt a slight tug on her rope. It was harder pulling him up than it was to let him down. Even though he was light in weight, she struggled against the gravity. David popped his head through the door, smiling at himself for his success.

"I think we can both go together. There's plenty of room

in here once you get in. I found a room where we can stop the pulley and get off. It's empty."

"It doesn't look that big, David. Suppose we can't control the pulley? What if we fall?"

"Oh, ye of little faith." He smiled as he reached for her hand. It was a tight fit, but it was exhilarating to be so close to her brother. She told herself to get rid of such thoughts and concentrate on the pulley. "Don't you want to see Dad?"

"Yes, I do, but . . . " Dana hesitated as she examined the ropes for tattered strands.

"But, what? Just get in here before the guard comes in to check on us!"

It was a slow, dark trip which they managed with some elbow jabs, quiet yelling, and a soft cheer of success as they stopped the dumbwaiter. There were no sounds behind the sliding access so it was presumably safe to enter. They jabbed each other until one was brave enough to raise the door, just an inch.

The room they were about to enter turned out to be the hotel's housekeeping department. They each nodded their approval. David was first to enter the room, deftly planting his feet on the floor. A sudden screech came from Dana, who was holding onto the ropes as tightly as she could wrestling against the pull of gravity and her own body weight.

David laughed as he pulled her out. Although she was disgusted with her brother for almost letting her drop to the bottom, she laughed along with him. These were the types of special moments she would always remember.

The lights were on in the large room, which meant there would soon be occupants. David rushed toward the entrance to investigate the hallway for clearance. With no one in sight, he signaled Dana to follow. Their adrenaline was flowing fiercely, their minds engrossed in their quest. They remained silent, stepping lightly through the corridors.

"What floor are we on?" Dana whispered.

"I'd guess the fifteenth by the number of doors we passed on the way down. Now, hush, woman!" David enjoyed taking charge on their excursions, leading the way to pending trouble, being a general nuisance to his sister.

The halls were silent, mainly due to everyone being ordered to remain in their rooms, although David could swear he heard footsteps behind them. While David looked behind him, Dana walked into his heels for she was following closely. The two looked at each other, ready to complain about their collision. Just then two men grabbed them and shoved them into an unoccupied room nearby.

As frightened as they were, Dana and David began kicking and screaming. The two men were prepared for their resistance and quickly covered their mouths with tape and tied their feet and hands. The ropes on Dana's wrists cut into her skin, causing a few tears to escape from her dark brown eyes. David gave her an "I'm sorry" look and tried to latch his fingers with hers to provide some comfort.

The men had thrown them into a closet, locking the door behind them. It happened so fast, neither had seen the men's faces. They heard feet shuffling across the carpet going away from the closet door, temporarily relieving them of any thoughts of being murdered at that moment.

"So what have we gotten ourselves into now?" one man shouted, banging something hard on a table top.

"Shut up, you ass! What if someone hears you?" The next few words were inaudible as the two men seemed to get farther away from the door. David was positive that these were the men who'd shot the guard earlier that day.

The closet was very dark but he could still see the outline of Dana's head. He felt guilty for dragging her with him, but he loved her very much and he would not have left the room without her. There surely would be an all-out search for them when their guard realized they are missing. It was the only thought that kept him calm.

It seemed as if several hours had gone by before someone opened the closet door, and Dana thought her bladder would explode. But as the two soon discovered only an hour had passed.

The man who opened the door was very short, grubby, and smiling strangely. "Do either of you have to use the 'toitie'?" Though his words seemed laden with sarcasm, he appeared to be sincere. Dana nodded several times, but David kept silent.

The man introduced himself. "My name is Manel." That was all he said before he untied Dana's feet and hands to lead her to the bathroom. Manel knew there was no means of escape so he let her go in by herself. As Manel and David waited for her, they stared at each other. "You know somethin'? You look just like your dad."

"Mmmblmm," was all David could say through the tape. He noticed the other man was not in the room.

"I'm sorry. I can't understand you with that tape there." Manel carefully removed the tape from David's mouth. David rubbed it several times, trying to get rid of the glue the tape left behind. His hands and feet were free; it felt good. "Now where is your sister?"

Manel knocked on the door, which quickly opened. Dana was standing there, tape on her mouth, sighing with relief. Manel proceeded to remove her tape as well. "I have to get you two back into the closet now."

Manel retied their hands and feet loosely and gave them the tapes for their mouths in case the door opened again and it was not their new friend. He gave them a small flashlight so they could see.

As soon as he shut the closet door, Lock returned—out

of breath and sweating. "Are they still in there?" Lock asked his partner, noticing how quickly Manel moved away from the door.

"Yes, they're still there! Where the hell do you think they'd go?" Manel was an expert at lying, but he seemed to feel bad about the abduction.

"I delivered the note. Those assholes should be acting on it at any moment. I noticed there was some commotion so they must have discovered the two kids were missing. Get ready, pal; we have to report to kitchen duty in ten minutes. We don't want to look suspicious, so get your butt moving."

David had heard every word, even over his sister's sobs. He heard a door slam but he could also hear some feet shuffling outside the closet door. Manel opened the door and gave them a single donut. As he shut the door, David tried to say thank you, but his voice was too soft for Manel to hear.

The flashlight was dim, but David could see the tears in Dana's eyes. He could never explain to anyone the pain he experienced in his stomach every time his sister cried. He loved his sister, but was this the way every brother felt?

David tried to smile through his glue-smeared face. Feeling awkward, he began to laugh. Dana followed, only she was laughing at his distorted smile. He reached for her hands and held them tightly. A warm, loving feeling swept through them as they held hands. David stared into her eyes, a look she knew all to well. David had always wanted to kiss her but knew he could not. She was a beautiful woman and also his sister.

Dana returned the same emotional look, her defenses down, her hopes limited. "What if they kill us?" she exclaimed, leaning toward him and embracing him, needing his strength.

"I won't let them do that to you!" David rubbed Dana's

arms to soothe her tense muscles. She tilted her head to him, enabling him to kiss her. "Are you sure?"

"Yes." She paused, knowing it was wrong, but she would never forgive herself if she did not let David know how she felt. They kissed lightly at first, testing the ground, making sure they were both in consent. Their hearts pounding, their hands shook as their long-awaited bonding took place. David kissed her passionately, his eyes closed but his soul combined with hers. Their kiss lasted for several minutes, heating them both, driving them to do something they were not ready for.

David pulled away softly yet forcefully, knowing his own weakness for his sister. "It's like a potato chip, you can't eat just one." Dana smiled up at him, her hair glowing in the light, her face delicately silhouetted against the closet wall. She leaned toward him again, slowly putting her arms around his waist, kissing him back with the same intensity they had felt before. This one lasted until they both fell asleep in each other's arms, silently loving each other, comforting themselves in a dangerous position.

CHAPTER 11

"Have you found them yet?" Phillip demanded of the guard just entering the room.

"No, sir. We're searching the entire hotel."

"Make sure you don't risk their lives in the process!"

Phillip could not concentrate on his own safety. His children were the most important people in his life. He sat for hours through the night, hoping to hear some good news. As each guard reported in person, no one had found any trace of Dana or David. Everyone was beginning to lose hope until early dawn, when Manel was caught in the kitchen stealing food. He claimed to be hungry and insisted that it was for himself. Phillip had seen the look in this man's eyes before, and his name bore an obvious relationship to the Manel he knew too well.

"Where are my children?" He startled even himself with the intensity of his voice.

"May I speak to you alone, sir?"

Phillip agreed, ordering one guard to stay by his side. "Come."

"Are you sure this is wise?"

Phillip reassured Manel that the guard would not repeat a word he said. "I hope you're right for your own sake." There was a hidden warning in Manel's words. Something was going to happen. "Talreja has changed. I have changed. Lock has also changed, but he is different than us." Manel showed fear of his long-time accomplice, emphasizing that the "new" Lock had no trouble walking or talking.

Manel certainly seemed different to Phillip. He was nice, but not overwhelmingly pushy. He seemed to be telling the truth, but how could he be trusted? *He is sincere,* the captain interrupted, not convinced his hasty decision was accurate.

"Why do you waste time explaining this to me?" Phillip's hands flew into the air. "Where are my children?"

"They are safe. I've taken good care of them." Manel hesitated, suspicious of the guard close by. "First, you must catch Lock." Manel gawked at the guard, knowing he had heard. "Lock said he was headed for the hotel's vault."

"What is in there that is so important to him?" Phillip thought Manel was being used as a decoy so as to assist Lock in his escape.

Manel answered honestly, proving himself worthy of Phillip's trust. "I don't know." He glanced at the table by his side that held the bag of food for Dana and David. "May I bring this to your children now? They must be starving."

"I'll send a guard with you. It's possible you are telling the truth, but I need to know that you are being watched. We'll take care of your partner." Phillip was determined to find Lock himself.

The guard who had been tricked by Dana and David followed Manel to his room. While Phillip discussed his plans with the remaining guards, the hotel manager left the kitchen to advise her employees to delay their duties until Lock was detained.

On the orders of his advisors, Phillip was brought back to the manager's office to be protected by two guards while the rest left for the vault. Phillip warned them to be wise; Lock was not an ordinary villain.

An hour passed before the guards returned. Lock did not accompany them. Their report was grim; still, Phillip knew Lock was around even though he was nowhere to be found. No documents or valuables had been stolen from the vault, which raised several questions among the group. Phillip demanded that his children be brought to him.

Manel took off running toward his room where Dana and David were being detained. The guard followed closely behind, thinking Manel was trying to get away. When they reached the door, Manel unlocked the closet and found Dana and David asleep, propped up against each other.

"Hey," Manel shouted, "are you two hungry?" He smiled as he unpacked the bag of food, watching them closely as the guard helped remove their loose bindings. Dana rubbed her wrists, which had been chafed during her confinement.

Even though the guard wanted to reprimand them for their earlier actions, he hugged them both, not realizing why he felt so attached to them. Manel had brought several donuts and a few cold pancakes from the kitchen. The guard, whom they now called Bud, told them to eat fast because their father wanted them by his side as soon as possible.

Dana and David had shared a terrifying experience, but they now realized the depths of their feeling for each other.

No one in the room they entered said one word as the family was reunited, keeping silent to avoid interrupting their joy. "I'm relieved that nothing happened to either of you. Dana, please let the nurse take care of that burn on your wrist as soon as we are done here. Did you eat?"

David had not minded the cold pancakes, but his appetite grew as he heard the breakfast menu. "Yes, but I think we could use something hot. Can I use the facilities?"

Phillip laughed and hugged David one more time before David left for the bathroom. "I don't want to keep you any longer, Dana. Please go with the nurse and get your wrist wrapped up."

"Thanks, Dad."

"For what? I didn't do anything. You have Bud to thank and, strangely enough, Manel." Phillip looked around the crowded room but Manel was not present. "Where did he go?"

Bud had locked the door to his room so Manel could not escape. "I'll bring him to you if you want, sir!" he said.

"That is not necessary. Manel will not be there when you arrive." Phillip waved his hand, signaling everyone to attend breakfast, ignoring Bud's obvious confusion. A frustrated Bud left the room, following Dana and David closer than he ever had before. "We'll discuss today's schedule while we eat." Phillip said.

Phillip was correct. Manel had vanished from his room, but it was an unexpected surprise to see him serving a special meal just for his children. Manel waited anxiously at the main dining room doors, ready to cater to their every wish.

Several major leaders requested information concerning the safety of themselves and their families. They were assured that all possible efforts were being made to secure the building. The security was overwhelming, each person being checked at every door for their identification badges. There were many discussions at each table concerning the continuance of the conference, which persuaded Phillip to make a preliminary announcement.

"The conference will continue. There is no need for concern. Please enjoy your meal. A formal announcement will follow." The diners in the other rooms were told of the announcement, not only to soothe their fears, but to allow Phillip to eat his well-deserved meal in peace.

I must speak to you, the captain whispered, absolutely unnecessarily.

Why now? Phillip had just begun to relax after the long night he'd been through.

There is no need for you to rise. Just listen.

Phillip waited for the captain to continue, pausing before he bit into a piece of bread. *Go ahead. Chew away. I can hear you.* Phillip's broad grin slowly appeared. Knowing his advisors were observing his moves much closer now, he continued to eat his meal. *I have a theory in reference to this recent fiasco. I don't believe your children were in any danger. I believe each scheme was a ploy to delay the conference.*

They tried to kill me! That's not a delay! Phillip was angry at the thought that his life, which was in danger, was considered to be a "casual delay."

Calm down! the captain roared. *It was fortunate they missed you! I believe Lock planned to eliminate you, thereby canceling the conference. I haven't been able to discover why Manel has changed. That, my friend, is a mystery.*

"Mr. President!" Phillip had not heard the first two addresses, making him hesitant to answer the third call.

"I do apologize." He wrapped his napkin around his fingers, wiping more than the food from his lips. "I have many things on my mind."

"We would appreciate your input on how to schedule the conference for today." His advisor understood how Phillip could be lost in his thoughts; he waited patiently for a response.

"We should follow yesterday's schedule. I realize this will delay us by one day, but it's extremely important for everyone to speak." Phillip thought for a moment, wondering how he could cram two days into one. "I believe if we shorten each speaker's time and work through the next two meals, we may fit everyone in before the evening is over."

"I'll propose this to the other dining halls if you will handle this one." His leading advisor, Hamilton, had always agreed with him, though many times he'd persuaded his president to take a different route toward his objectives.

The moment full approval was received by every major leader, the conference resumed. Many had been forced to adjust their speeches to allow their major concerns to be heard within the specific time.

Phillip stood behind the podium once again. With more protection beside him, he continued. "As you all were given the order in which your speeches will be given, I do emphasize that time is extremely important due to yesterday's events. Everyone must be given an opportunity to speak."

There were few arguments as to the order of speeches, but no one came forward.

The speeches began, hurriedly. Everyone had valid complaints and wishes, which were, at times, dramatic and whiny. Eyes began to water, heads began to nod, one man snoring in the far right rear jolted awake as a crisp gavel struck the podium. It was announced that the conference would resume the next day.

Phillip returned to his room to find Dana and David sleeping on the couch. They had been waiting for him to return for several hours. Bud had spent the entire evening with them, listening to their views of how the world should be.

"They are extremely intelligent, Mr. President," Bud whispered softly, trying not to disturb their sleep. "There are few children who admire their parents as much as yours do you. I'm sorry your wife cannot be here."

"She is, Bud, she is."

Phillip stared at the two slumped bodies on the couch. Not wanting to disturb them, he lightly covered them with a blanket. Bud dropped wearily into a chair to guard them.

Phillip's bedroom was dark except for the street lights shining through his window. A single candle was lit, as he had not done that morning, for Felicia. He spoke to her of the day's events, told her he loved her, and retired for the night. Even the captain could not reach him. Phillip was exhausted and fell into a deep sleep.

CHAPTER 12

The following days of the conference proved to be successful. Many major leaders reached agreements to further the project financially and provide manpower to the smaller countries in their environmental clean-up. The entire conference lasted for six days, the seventh day being dedicated to an afternoon gathering before each leader and their families returned home.

The hotel had been decorated during the early morning hours to prepare for the celebration. All chefs had been busy preparing certain lavish dishes, which were not served during the regular meals that week.

Before the celebration began, Phillip gave a memorial speech for the guard who had been murdered. He did not dwell on the fact that the guard was murdered; instead, he had sent for the guard's family the previous day, inviting them to join the ceremony. The guard's body was scheduled to return with his wife and children to their home shortly after Phillip's eulogy.

They had been invited to stay for the gathering, but it was not the time for them to celebrate—even if the conference's purpose was for the good of the world. As far as the guard's family was concerned, their world had been destroyed the moment they lost their father and beloved husband. Phillip understood the wife's pain more than she realized.

As a few guards escorted the grieving family from the

hotel, Phillip watched, noticing the wife had been staring at him until she received his attention. She waved to him, thanking him for his thoughtfulness; then she turned and left. Phillip felt an emptiness he never expected. The lost look in the woman's eyes reminded him of the day Felicia had died, bringing back many forgotten memories.

Dana knew where her father's mind had wandered. She thought of her mother as well as David. As always, their thoughts were interrupted.

A band had been scheduled to play during the celebration, making it possible for certain requests for songs throughout the world to be performed. Each band member wore a black suit and white shirt, except for one stranger who sat beside the stage. This strangely dressed man stepped on the stage to replace the musician seated at the piano. Phillip listened to the jovial music the man played, a song he had never heard before. As he walked closer to the stage, he suddenly stopped and began to smile.

Manel had taken over the piano, singing and banging out a song he had written a few days before. His song was about two children, a boy and a girl, who were friends for their entire lives. As the song progressed, there was a chorus he repeated, sending Phillip's thoughts into total confusion and worry. The chorus began, "They were friends and pals, always to be together, never knowing their identities; they were friends then lovers, always remembering their priorities."

Manel was clearly not meant to be a poet, but he played the piano as if he were the keys. His melody was easy to dance to and required a great amount of energy. David asked his sister to dance, offering his hand to lead her to the dance floor. They were not listening to the words of the song, but felt the rhythm of the music through their feet as they moved between the crowd of dancers.

When are you planning to tell them? The captain was concerned, for Manel knew Phillip's secret.

I should have told them several years ago. I know that I have made a mistake, but Felicia and I agreed not to tell them.

Phillip watched his children as they danced through two more songs Manel had written. He planned to tell them his secret when they returned home. It was not the time or place to relieve his thoughts.

As the afternoon progressed, several families returned to their rooms, packing their belongings and saying good-bye to the friends they had made. There was a deeper meaning to the conference than the environmental issue. Many people had exchanged addresses, hoping to keep in contact with one another. Someday they would see each other again.

Manel wished a safe trip home to the two new friends he had made. The fact that Manel had come so close to Dana and David disturbed Phillip even though the captain reassured him Manel meant no harm.

To Phillip, the trip home seemed longer than he had anticipated, thinking about how he was going to tell his children the truth. He imagined several ways, trying to think of the right places, the right time and the right words. *For this, my friend, there is no right place, time or words. You must speak to them alone.* Phillip always had taken the captain's words to heart, knowing that he knew more about Phillip than Phillip himself.

Home. It was always nice to return home even if an exciting trip had been taken. Phillip told his children to meet him in the library after they were settled. They had eaten dinner on the jet, but he promised them a dessert from the kitchen before they retired. Even as grown up as his "children" were, they would always appreciate the night-time snacks he used to sneak them.

David stopped before his bedroom door to watch Dana as she struggled with her bags down the corridor. He began to laugh at her. "Don't laugh, you idiot! Help me!" Dana always packed too much, which David had never understood until this recent trip. He had run out of shirts and underwear several times during the past week, making him realize he was not a very organized person.

"Do you need help unpacking?" he asked her sincerely, knowing all he had to do was dump the contents of his suitcase into the laundry bin.

"No, but thanks for the offer," Dana smiled as she placed one hand on her cheek. "I'll meet you in the library as soon as I'm finished here." Her door shut, leaving David bewildered.

He wondered if she had something in her suitcases she did not want him to see. For once, he respected her privacy and entered his freshly cleaned room. *Now that I'm here, I can get this place back to normal!* he thought. David was not a slob, but he did not like his room to be perfect and orderly. He waited to hear Dana's door open so he could walk with her to the library. He could not think of any specific reason; he only felt he had to.

Dana surprised him as she stood at his door, "You're old enough to pick up after yourself." She tried her best to be serious, but they laughed together as they headed for the library. They never knew that Bud had listened to the entire conversation from his adjacent room. Once they were out of hearing range, he burst into laughter.

Phillip had started a fire in the fireplace to warm the room, thinking the atmosphere would help his nerves. He did not know what reaction he would receive in a short while; all he knew was that this was going to be the hardest thing he had ever done in his life. He wished Felicia was with him at this moment, for she had always given him strength to do almost anything.

"We're here," both children announced as they entered the library.

The fire lit up the room, spitting and sparking as the logs took flame.

"The fire is nice, Dad." Dana always enjoyed the fireplace, especially at Christmastime. It seemed to give her a warm and comfortable feeling inside.

"There's some pie for each of you on the table, if you wish. I had the cook make some hot chocolate as well." Phillip pointed to the small table, which held their sugar high for the evening.

"Oh, is this a bribe?" David joked with his father, not realizing he was correct.

"What do you want to tell us?" Dana asked, realizing her father was not laughing at David's comment.

Phillip paced back and forth in front of the fireplace, eventually seating himself in his favorite chair next to Dana and David. "What I am about to tell you is very difficult. Please be patient with me." He paused as the captain gave him strength to continue. "Your mother loved you both very much. I wish she could be here with us, but as it turns out, I must do this alone." He held his hands in his lap, grasping them harder than he realized.

"When we were married, we decided to wait a few years before starting a family. Felicia was very young and not ready for the responsibility that comes with child rearing. But finally the time came when we decided we were ready for such a drastic change in our lives." Phillip sipped his coffee cautiously, realizing it was burning his lips. He continued as he set his cup on the table beside his chair. "When your mother was pregnant with you, Dana, there were several complications. She almost lost her life giving birth. We were very lucky you both survived the ordeal.

"We wanted to have more children, but fate seemed to have other plans. The doctor advised against another pregnancy. He was positive that your mother would not survive another childbirth." Phillip kept a close watch on David, realizing the last piece of pie he had just eaten was still in his mouth.

"Your mother and I discussed this at length. We spent many nights arguing, but we finally decided to try another route."

David finally swallowed the chunk of pie in his mouth.

"David, you are my son and your mother's son, even though we did not create you as we did Dana. There was a teenage girl who had become pregnant and was planning to get an abortion. Your mother and I knew her for several years before your birth. She never told us who the father was and we felt it was not our business to pry. She assured us that the man was not ill in any way and that there would be no question about a healthy child.

"We decided it was best not to tell you until you were older and would understand our situation. I can't introduce you to your real mother because, sadly, she died during your delivery. We both held her hand as she pushed for the last time and quietly passed away."

Dana's eyes were filled with tears, feeling her father's pain, his voice trembling as he spoke.

"I apologize if I have done wrong by both of you for not telling you sooner. I hope you understand why we kept it from you. If you need to speak from your heart and let me know what you're feeling, please do not hold back for my sake." Phillip was relieved to have finished, feeling as if he had taken another turn in his life, making him feel complete.

David ran to his father and hugged him harder than he

had ever done before. Dana joined in, making it a three-way hug. The tears flowed from their eyes, tears of joy and frustration. "I love you, Dad. It's okay," David soothed his father's fears, understanding the decision his parents had made. David never asked why his birth mother had become pregnant; some things were better off left unsaid.

"I know you're both very tired. Please go to your rooms and we'll do whatever you want in the morning. Yes, I admit that I feel guilty, but I feel better now that you know the truth."

They kissed their father good-night, smiled at him, and left him in the library by himself. Phillip needed time alone to gather his thoughts before he retired for the evening.

When Dana and David reached their rooms, Bud was listening to them in the hall. He heard them crying, but he felt it was best not to disturb them.

"I love you, Dana," David managed to say through his tears as he hugged her.

"I love you, too."

It was a long night. All three had difficulty falling asleep. Eventually the energy they had used while crying made them weary.

CHAPTER 13

Phillip decided not to run for president at the next election, much to the disappointment of his supporters. He was tired and felt he needed to spend more time with his family. During his last term as president, the country's economy strengthened; it was better than originally estimated. He was proud of his accomplishments throughout the past several years.

The Environment Awareness Conference had taken several years to become a success. Many Third World countries had become economically secure, seldom dependent upon adjacent countries, but there were still many disputes within each country concerning the amount of funds allocated to help others.

As always, not everyone agreed with the new way of the world. *That's what makes the world so interesting,* Phillip thought to himself as he watched the evening news. His private phone had been ringing several times before he picked up the receiver. It was Dana, wishing him a happy birthday. She always made time to call him now that she lived by herself. He was shocked when he heard David's voice wishing him a happy one as well.

"Where are you two?" Phillip had not thought Dana and David had seen each other much after they'd moved away.

David responded, "I'm at Dana's apartment. Do you think she would leave it up to me to remember your birthday? She practically tied me up!" He heard his father laugh, knowing that he knew David's memory was terrible.

"This is a nice surprise! While I have you both on the phone, when are you planning to visit?" As a father would, he needed to see his children.

"We plan to come next month after you return from Hawaii. Is that all right?" David sensed the urgency in his father's voice.

"Don't worry." He sighed "There's nothing wrong. I'm as healthy as I ever was. It's fine to come next month. I wouldn't be able to spend much time with you before I leave, so it's best we wait."

Phillip caught up on his children's lives, asking them questions about who they were dating and how their employers were treating them. All of his questions were answered in detail except for the first one.

"I don't know about Dana, but I've been so busy at work I haven't had time to need anyone."

Dana replied the same, changing the subject to avoid any more questions.

"How are you? We've been keeping up with the news reports, but we want to hear the actual stories from you." Phillip had volunteered as a traveling advisor to continue his quest for a healthy world environment.

"You can hear my stories when I return. Now get off the phone before you run up your bill!"

Phillip heard the captain request his attention. Using the phone bill as an excuse, he said his good-byes and slowly put the receiver back on its stand.

We're getting old, my friend, the captain agreed although he was not aging like Phillip. *What's on your mind?*

As you know, we have not discovered why your life has gone in this direction. I admit I've been foiled! Do you have any thoughts on this subject?

No.

Phillip was weary from the day's activities, but it helped to close his eyes as he spoke to his friend. *I have not received any threats or tasks in a few years. Have "they" gone away?*

I don't think so. You are falling asleep. The captain changed the subject quickly knowing that Phillip's body needed to rest. *Fall asleep, my friend. I'll join you in your dreams. It's much more enjoyable to speak to you face to face.* No sooner had he finished, then Phillip was snoring away.

For the first time, the captain was blocked from entering Phillip's first dream. It was not until his third attempt that he was able to enter.

You must have a lot on your mind. It took me a while to get in.

You're lucky you weren't successful. As Phillip sat in the sand, he breathed heavily as if he had been exhausted by his first two dreams. *They are still here, Cap'.*

You seem disturbed. What happened? The captain sat beside Phillip, joining him to watch the waves of the ocean dream.

I wasn't sure at first, but it came clear to me that "Satan," as we had thought he was, entered my dream. He paused, wringing his fingers.

What do you mean by that? The captain changed positions as one of his legs became numb.

We have been tricked, and I must say it was quite successful. Phillip could not explain fast enough for the captain. *The first thing I remember, I entered a church, which was quite old by its appearance. There was an angel or something waiting for me at the other end of the church. The voice was obvious, but he or she did not reveal their true identity.*

What was said to you?

Phillip frowned as he tried hard to remember the exact words he had heard. *All I can remember is that the angel said that God was proud of me for the work I have done during my life. The next thing I know, I was floating but I did not have a body.*

The captain replied, *Go on.* He knew exactly where Phillip had gone, but he had no right to tell him where he'd actually been.

In the second dream I was with my children. I heard crying in the background, but I could not see who was making such a fuss.

I don't know what your dreams mean. I'm sorry, but I can't help you. The captain was lying but he realized he had no right to tell Phillip.

I'm so tired these days. I realize I travel all over the world, but I'm still young at heart!

Give yourself time. You've done so many things in your life that it's not surprising you're tired! Do rest. I'll speak to you again.

Phillip slept.

CHAPTER 14

"Should we call him to see if he's all right?" Dana was concerned about their father, watching him do so much for others, but not doing anything for himself as he'd promised.

"We must tell him when he returns." David held her hand close to his heart as they delayed their departure from the warm bed. "I hope he understands this. I couldn't bear to think if we never told him and we lost him . . . "

"Don't say that! He's still in good health, and you're scaring me!"

David kissed Dana lightly on her lips, whispering to her how much he loved her. "I can't help but think that we never would have become so close if we were not stuck together so much! I'm glad you've always been there for me." David smiled and kissed her again.

"Is this right? I mean for us to love each other this way?" Dana was concerned religiously as well as morally.

"I love you with all my heart. That, my sweet, is enough for the 'man upstairs.'" He paused to kiss her shoulder, lightly pushing her hair to the side.

"Dad will be home tomorrow, and I'm sure he's busy completing his paperwork before he returns. Besides, we have the next three weeks off, so let's enjoy each other." They fell back asleep, holding each other in their arms.

His plane landed on time, relieving Dana and David of the worry about an "accident." Their father was safely home, feeling refreshed and full of energy due to the success of the oil-spill clean-up. It had been a small one, but who knew a meteor would hit the ship?

They watched everyone come through the gate as the plane unloaded and luggage was transported. There he was, tan, smiling, and running toward his children with outstretched arms. They enjoyed their three-way hugs several times.

Dana had rented a limousine, knowing her father had not had the pleasure of riding in one for several years. David played with all the gadgets, turning the television on and off, opening and closing the refrigerator door, and turning switches, having no idea what they were for. "Stop your constant fiddling!" Phillip exclaimed, exasperated. "We're almost home so clean up this mess! I can't believe you two are still so childish."

"Yes, dear!" David was sarcastic, but he meant it in a loving way.

"What's up with you two? Haven't you stopped bickering yet?" Phillip clapped his hand on David's leg, startling him, which made him drop an unopened can of beer. "Sorry about that, son!" Laughter roared through the vehicle as David opened the can of beer. Everyone was wet and sticky, even the driver.

"You idiot! Everyone knows that you don't open a dropped or shaken can." Dana could never understand David's thinking.

"Oh, get a grip, Dana!"

Both were very tense, realizing that they were almost home and their secret would be revealed to the man they had admired and loved their entire lives.

The house Phillip had purchased after his political career ended was small enough for him, but it could handle a few overnight guests. The yard had been taken care of by a lawn service. The house had been watched by a neighbor who, also alone, had become close friends with Phillip over the past few years.

Phillip had a special seat on his porch which he spent hours in, reading books and designing plans for his EA group.

"Please, sit down. You can both unpack later. Tell me what you've been doing!"

Dana looked at David, hoping he would begin telling their father the news. "Dad, we have something to tell you, but we aren't sure how you're going to react."

"Remember, I said the same thing to you both many years ago? Spit it out now. I'm sure it can't be that bad." Phillip's hand slammed down on the arm of his chair, almost loosening the old wood that held it in place.

"Dana and I were married three months ago." There! He'd said it flat out. David watched his father look at him then at Dana. No positive reaction, just a stare. "Dad? Are you all right?"

"Yes." He laughed. "I expected this to happen." He held out his arms to hug them, which they readily obliged.

"There's something else." Dana's eyes were shining with happiness, knowing that her father was difficult to shock. "By Christmastime, you'll be a grandfather."

No other time except his marriage to Felicia and the birth of his children had made him happier than he was at this moment. "My dear little girl is going to have a little one herself! I'm going to be a grandfather? Now I feel really old!"

The three hugged and laughed all afternoon, listening to their father's stories and watching Dana run to the bathroom every half hour. "She's pukin', Dad. I can't believe how much she pukes!"

"David, there are other words than 'puke.' Don't tease her. She'll need as much support during the next seven months ahead as you can give her. Be patient. You'll be rewarded once the baby comes." He felt uneasy referring to his children as parents, but he had expected it to happen and the shock was not as great as they had thought it would be.

Dana had stopped working two weeks before she delivered a beautiful baby girl. They named her Felicia, after their mother. This brought tears to Phillip's eyes every time he held his granddaughter.

Dana, David, and Felicia visited their father for the Christmas holiday. Felicia was only two weeks old, sleeping in her grandfather's arms as he rocked her in his living room chair. The fireplace was lit, heating the entire house. Phillip offered to take the early morning feeding so David and Dana could get some well-deserved rest. As Felicia slept soundly in his arms, Phillip began to fall asleep as well.

Phillip, my love. In his dream, her voice was clear and pure. Felicia, his wife, accompanied the captain as they walked along the shoreline. It had been too many years since he had hugged his beloved wife.

Phillip stared at the captain, asking with his eyes how this could be real? The captain nodded, shrugged, and continued to walk away. The last words he heard the captain say would stay in his memory forever.

You don't need me anymore, my friend. It's time for me to go. Enjoy what precious time you have with your wife. Good-bye, my son.

Phillip would not let Felicia escape from his arms as she tried to speak to him. He told her to be patient, he needed to feel her soul against his for as long as he could.

I must go soon, my love. Please let me speak. Reluctantly, he released his hold, but he held her hand as they walked along the water's edge. *I'm here to guide Felicia, our granddaughter. She is lovely, isn't she?*

Yes, my love. Tell me, why have you been sent to guide her?

I can't say because I don't know. I only know that we will see each other again some day when I am finished. Be patient, my love. She kissed him for a long time, as long as time itself permitted.

His dream had ended. Felicia slept soundly in his arms until she became hungry once again.

Dana lay restless in her bed, wondering why Felicia had been crying for such a long time. "I know Dad is familiar with her feeding times. Why doesn't he feed her?"

David was still half-asleep, moaning and mumbling for her to bring Felicia to him. Felicia wailed even louder as Dana entered the room. Phillip held his granddaughter tightly. Too tight.

"David! David! Come here!" He got there as fast as he could, after first picking himself up off the floor. He had fallen out of bed when Dana screamed.

"He's gone, David! He's gone!"

The day was filled with tears and several visits from neighbors close by. Dana could not bear to be away from Felicia; she held her every second of the day.

It was a beautiful ceremony, with almost three thousand people attending.

Phillip was to be buried next to his wife the following day. It took almost all morning for David to coerce Dana into leaving Felicia with one of the ladies who lived near their father's house. Phillip's body was being transported by plane to the burial ground. Dana gave Felicia a warm and loving kiss, as did David, and reluctantly entered the car that would take them to the airport.

Phillip, their beloved father, was finally at peace, placed alongside his wife forever.

CHAPTER 15

"White." All he could see was "white." He spun himself around. *Where the hell am I?*

On the contrary. You are in Purgatory. The place between Heaven and Hell.

Who are you? Am I dead?

You already know who I am. Yes, you have ended your life on Earth. You have a new beginning.

Why can't I see my body?

You need no such thing here or where you may go.

I have so many questions to ask. Will you answer them?

As long as you have questions, I will answer.

He thought long and hard, trying to ask several questions at once, except that one question kept repeating itself to him.

No. It was not "Satan" as you perceive him.

How did you know what I was going to ask?

I can hear your thoughts.

Oh. That was no surprise to him. He continued. *Why was my wife taken from me?*

She was not taken from you, only her body was taken. It was her time to leave.

Time? What is that supposed to mean? We would have had so many wonderful years together!

She has always been a part of you. She can never leave you.

He knew he had more questions to ask. He let his first

one slip into the back of the list, planning to ask it again later. *Who were Manel, Talreja, and Lock?*

They were sent to push you in the right direction.

Oh. He did not completely understand the answer, but he continued. *Why was one of my guards shot instead of me?*

It was his time.

May I ask you more questions?

I will answer them as long as you ask them.

He thought carefully about his next question, taking his time now that he knew this "voice from nowhere" would not leave him. *Why was I chosen to have a guardian? Where is the captain?*

It was important to keep you alive to succeed in your goals. The captain is in Heaven.

His questions were becoming easier. *Why was he assigned to me?*

That I cannot answer.

Why? Phillip had thought if he asked a question, it would be answered.

I have answered you. It was not stated that each question would receive an explanation.

Oh. This "voice" was highly intelligent and knew exactly how to answer his multitude of questions. *Then I can assume I will never know why?*

Yes.

Does the captain know why?

No. He will never know. Do you have another question? The voice knew very well he had more to ask. Phillip decided to oblige and change his direction of questioning.

Where am I going?

When?

When I'm done asking questions.

Heaven.

Phillip was lucky to enter directly into Heaven, but he

needed to know the reason why. *What have I done to deserve such an honor?*

You have made the Earth a better place to live for your children and others.

I thought Purgatory was a place where you suffered for your sins?

It is.

He was confused. He had not suffered yet, and he did not wish to. *What were my sins in life?*

Why don't you tell me?

He thought again. When had he ever done anything against God or his religion? Phillip knew there must be at least one sin he had committed. It disturbed him that he could not remember, for sins were considered to be a permanent mark on your memory until you achieved something good to be forgiven for that sin. *I understand! Since I fought to make the world a better place, I have destroyed the memory of my sins.*

You are correct. Do you have more questions?

Is there a Santa Claus? Phillip needed to break the monotony of questions running through his mind.

You do have a sense of humor, don't you? Santa Claus existed but not as children are made to believe. It is a feeling inside you of giving and thankfulness for what you receive. There was a certain Santa Claus many, many of your years ago.

When my children brought me their request to stop a war, why was I given the opportunity to see what the result might have been?

You know the answer. They did not go, did they?

Phillip realized his questions were becoming stale. He must think of more. Thinking of his parents he decided to ask a simple question. *Where are my mother and father?*

They are in Heaven.

What is Heaven? He knew he might not receive an answer, but decided to try.

That, I cannot answer.

As expected. He needed to ask more questions, ones that he knew could be answered. *When I was given the task of abolishing bigotry, I wondered if my ideas would make a difference. Will mankind continue to work together?*

That is an answer I cannot give. I must tell you only one aspect of this problem. It will only work if bigotry dies with the people who harbor it. It is up to the children to fight the disease.

Disease? I never thought of it as a disease. He waited a while for an answer, but he received more than expected.

It's catchy. Anyone can come down with it if they are subjected to many people who are infected. As with AIDS, if one person does not have it, no one will.

How did the disease exist if the first person who was infected didn't receive it from someone else?

That I cannot answer. No one can.

Phillip thought about this reply. *No one can answer?* This was one question that only the human race could answer. He would not dwell on the subject any further.

What about the decrease in taxes?

That was Talreja's idea. He was not told to do so.

What? Phillip was angry at the thought that a "messenger" would play with his life.

Please be calm. His ancestors had been tortured for non-payment of taxes to their lords. It was his way of getting back at the world.

When I was young, how did I survive all those "close call" accidents?

That is why the captain was sent to you. However, it was a very difficult decision to let him contact you. This is only done on rare occasions. There have been too many souls destroyed by society for hearing "voices," some of which were evil voices making them do evil things. Most were only being protected, but they were frightened by the contact.

Why do I feel exhausted?

It is because you are exhausting your soul. Too many questions, not enough answers. Your soul is frustrated.

I feel the need to be somewhere. Why?

You are being "called" by someone.

I have no more questions.

Then I will go.

Phillip?

Felicia, his beloved wife, appeared before his eyes. *Come with me, my love!* She held his hand, pulling him with her. He felt himself "fade" into her.

As their souls combined into one, their love energized. A bright light flashed in the center, pulling them in its direction. A soothing "white." A peaceful love they had never experienced before—or had they?